PRAISE FOR THE IRISH EDITION OF
TAR AND FEATHERS

"Impressive and utterly compelling."
—Kate Cruise O'Brien, *Image Magazine*

"A vivid and disturbing rendition of family life."
—*Oxford Times*

"Ms. Nelson can write like an angel or a devil, which ever way one wishes to regard it. . . . As a chronicler of the quiet desperation of much of modern life, she is equal to the best."
—Vincent Lawrence, *Sunday Press*

OTHER BOOKS BY DOROTHY NELSON

In Night's City

TAR AND FEATHERS

DOROTHY NELSON

DALKEY ARCHIVE PRESS
NORMAL · LONDON

First U.S. edition, 2004

Library of Congress Cataloging-in-Publication Data

Nelson, Dorothy, 1948–
Tar and feathers / Dorothy Nelson.— 1st Dalkey Archive ed.
p. cm.
ISBN: 1-56478-373-1 (acid-free paper)
1. Problem families—Fiction. 2. Mothers and sons—Fiction. 3. Abused wives—Fiction. 4. Ex-convicts—Fiction. 5. Ireland—Fiction. I. Title.

PR6064.E52T37 2004
823'.914—dc22

2004053773

Partially funded by grants from the Lannan Foundation and the Illinois Arts Council, a state agency.

Dalkey Archive Press is a nonprofit organization located at Milner Library (Illinois State University) and distributed in the UK by Turnaround Publisher Services Ltd. (London).

www.centerforbookculture.org

Printed on permanent/durable acid-free paper and bound in the United States of America.

Blackness crept forth from the
forest and at once I thought, this
will not end well . . . Oh, what howling
and whistling around the house, how the trees
are jeering . . . How the wind outside is
worrying the forest

Werner Herzog
Of Walking in Ice

PART I

Salt And Pepper On Their Heads

The day broke out into a purple colour. Long ribbon-like streamers dart around the air loose and friendly, running down people's faces and curving in a halo around their heads and they don't even know it. I giggle, nobody likes me giggling, they say, 'What are you to you?', or, 'You're stupid' in big sucking voices as if they are sick to death of me. When I giggle they know I keep a secret from them because I never tell anyone what I see. I hold secrets inside me like kisses I can't let out. I want to kiss everyone but a boy can't, he can only say, 'Hallo how's things?' Hallo, hallo, hallowed be thy name. You see, you see, everyone prays when they see you but they won't kiss in case they get a big disease, or something, because your mouth carries germs and you might die or get sick. That's why we all shake hands, it doesn't matter because we can't feel anything but we won't die.

I creep around the town like a mouse keeping in close to the walls and my face as ordinary looking as I can make it. I try to look as though I could be anyone so you wouldn't recognise me in a lineup. I wanted to wear a balaclava but it's too theatrical. I wouldn't mind getting caught, I'd like to go to court just to see what it's like because I love plays. I see a lot of plays on television and once or twice I went to a real theatre. Da use to play 'Judge' with me all the time. His dream was for me to tell the truth to everyone and to turn out honest as the day is long. That's silly that is. He used to send me into the sitting room and ten minutes later he'd come in and sit opposite me. Then he'd interrogate me.

'Where were you?'

'Who were you out with?'

'Were you near the chemist between two and four when it was broken into?'

'You say you weren't there and yet you say you can't remember where you were. Don't look, what colour jumper have you got on? You know that well enough, so don't tell me you don't know where you were between two and four.'

'Where were you between six and seven last Thursday when the vegetable shop was broken into?'

I sat in the chair with a look on my face as if to say I'm broken-hearted you even think it was me. You should always look sorry for yourself in the docks otherwise they'll call you a know-all and up your sentence for cheek. The judges on the telly wear wigs and cloaks whereas my Da wore his old shirt and trousers, he's no style at all. If I end up in court I'll do something dramatic like not recognising it the way political prisoners do. Martin Thompson a friend of mine from school said he heard a man saying no one had the right to judge you. It was a discussion about women having abortions and he said it was the most brilliant thing he'd ever heard anyone say. It was exactly what I intended to say if I ever got caught. I've done most of the shops around the town, well you have to if you want to be anything. Between one and two Mr Robinson the sweet shop man goes next door to the pub, gets a bottle of guinness and a sandwich, it takes him about four minutes to get back again. You have to stand around the full hour because if he's busy he won't leave the counter. And sometimes he has this girl come in, maybe she's his daughter, she looks a bit like him anyway. On good days I stuff my jacket and trouser pockets with bars of sweets. I don't take chocolates, they melt quick as ice cream does in the summer. And on bad days I get wet if its raining, or just fed up waiting on the old man to make his mind up. The bad luck of it is that four minutes doesn't give me enough time to get in behind the counter and do the cash register. But never mind I can't have everything. After that I meet all the lads in the cafe on the main street and we play records and eat the sweets.

Sometimes I manage twenty cigarettes as well because they're at the end of the counter just behind the flap. I'm a chain smoker and Mam's always begging me to give them up for her sake. Why should I? I love sitting with all the lads, though to tell you the truth some of the things they do make me sick. One lad has a crowbar and his friend has a knuckle duster and they go down to the toilets on the seafront and wait for someone to come in. If he's able to crawl back out it's his lucky day. I'm dead against violence myself, I suppose that makes me a pacifist of some sort. I'm too small and skinny to take anyone on but let me stand beside you for ten seconds and you won't notice your wallet is missing. I gave up nicking things for Lent last year but it nearly killed me. I got these terrible headaches and I felt as if I was going to be sick all the time. I suppose I was suffering from withdrawal symptoms. Maybe next year I'll give up smoking and see how that goes.

My Ma sits by the window her hair turning gold with the light shining on it and she goes into a trance and speaks out to an invisible crowd. – 'Jesus went forth into the mountains to slay himself a goose, whereupon he plucked the feathers out one by one. Moving deeper into the mountainside he left a trail of light white feathers for the ones behind. You think he suffered there don't you? Contemplating what lay behind and what the future held in store for him, two brown eggs by the finest hen lay in wait for our man. The poor man suffered all right. Consider the ashes of Redemption, imagine coming across a pile such as that late at night when you are already exhausted. Those who are expecting God always want to touch him and Jesus was no exception,' she said.

She snaps out of the trance like a twig underfoot, click, she throws her head back, her throat as crumpled as the walls of a cave, her hand circling it lightly, her laugh coarse as sandpaper, her eyes gleaming liquid thoughts, dark and overflowing as if they'll burst through her eyes any second and her neck will crack but no –

'Bring me a basin of warm water,' she instructs.

I wash and dry her hands in the basin of water carefully.
'Put the kettle on for me,' she instructs next.
She smokes and sips the hot tea.
'How was it?' she asks.
'It was fine,' I say.
'Did you think it went down well?'
'Smashing I'd say.'
'Good. Some days it goes better then others.'
She comes up behind me and puts her arm around me, draws me into her and kisses the back of my head.
'You're growin' up into a fine, fine lad,' she says.

My Ma and Da cooed like wood pigeons across the table to each other every morning.
'Cooey lovey.'
'Yes lovey.'
'I love you lovey.'
'I know. I know lovey.'
'Cooey, cooey.'
'Yes dear.'
'I still love you lovey.'
'I still love you too lovey.'
'Cooey.'
'Yes love.'
'Now do you still love me?'
'Of course lovey, of course.'
'That's good and you.'
'I love you forever lovey.'
'You're sure about that?'
'Of course I'm sure lovey.'
'That's a relief.'
'And now?'
'Yes lovey.'
And when she went upstairs he missed her so much he shouted up through the ceiling.
'Are you alright up there? What's keepin' you so long?'

She came flying out to the top of the stairs and shouted down to him.

'What did you say?'

When she came back down you could hear the rustle of her silk slip on the stairway. Its cool blue colour against her marble coloured skin. She smelt like fresh hay when she stepped into the kitchen. She blew me a kiss across the crowded room and I bore a laser beam stare into his large round pink balding skull. – Get out Da. Get out. But he ignored me.

When they first got married everyone said, 'Good luck to the pair of you. I hope you have a long and happy life' and shook a box of confetti over them. Then he lifted her up in his arms and carried her off into the sunset. His jet black hair had a greasy sheen to it and as she lay her arm across his broad strong shoulders she gasped at the strength of him. The muscles in his arms rippled under his wedding suit as he smiled down on his bride and he took a tulip and gave it to her. She lay it across her heart weak with love for him.

'I love you,' she whispered in his ear. 'Oh how I love you.'

He set her tenderly down by his side and clenching his fist in a victory salute they chorused together, 'Up yours' in memory of my granny who didn't think he was the right man for her.

Now he snored in short quick bursts followed by a gasp for air and then a long trailing snore like a snail along the ground and she sat snug and contented in the chair opposite wrapped in the warmth of his sleep like a blanket. I saw them happy and I put that in a corner of my mind so I'd never forget. I saw them happy as a swing rocking slowly in the summer breeze, sometimes creaking with rust and iron age, then curving upwards in a sweep towards the sky, a happy beam of wood. I saw them happy and all day I am too as if happiness spreads like sunshine to the four corners of the earth. How will I remember everything that ever happened and give it back to them with my love when their brains dry up with old age and she says take no notice of him he's gone senile, but it's really her. Oh she turned and gave me a long sultry stare, her dark brown eyes full of hidden messages.

She looked bruised and wounded as if she had been through hell and back. Oh how sultry she looked with her mouth dipping down at the corners and pouting at me like that.

It was against her principles to smile. Even when she was smoking she looked as if she was sending out secret messages, her sad face barely visible behind the curling spiral of smoke, her elbow on the table, her hand cupped under her chin and her long slim fingers spread like a fan across her cheek. I looked like her. Sometimes I sat in front of her dressing table practising all her different expressions. She was beautiful and she was such a shining tragedy because we were poor and she was made for better things. I really love tragedy. I hope she had a terrible life before, maybe waiting for a true love that never turned up, or she married Da on the rebound and right from the start he made her miserable. Then she waited for me to turn up and here I am and I don't even know what to say to her sometimes. For instance when he went on the dole she sat stiff and upright in the chair, so regal and haughty with disappointment and he blushed with shame at having let her down again. You see, you see, I don't know what to say to her.

And last night, she thought to herself, they said things are getting worse. Another factory closed down, the biggest yet, they said. Five hundred men let go in one week. The other government said if we vote for them next time they'll make a quarter of a million jobs in one year. The other government said that's nonsense, you can't do that. The other government said that what's wrong is this government doesn't know how to run the country. The other government said it goes back six years when the other government was in. And you're holier than thou I suppose the other government said. The other government said food prices will have to go up this week and the other government said if they were in food prices wouldn't go up this week. The other government said we've no choice but to put them up. The other government said that's nonsense the trouble with you is you've no heart. The other government said it was hard to credit what the other government said because they were doing their best. The other government said my heart goes out to all those people who are suffering. The other government said they'd done nothing when they were in but their heart was going out to all those poor people who were suffering while they were having to do what they didn't do then, the other government said. On the telly people went out on a march to protest to the government that they weren't going to be the ones to pay for the government's mistakes. But the mistakes were the other government's, the government said.

My Da walked quickly down the main steet, turned at Neary's corner up into Heaneys street and headed home past the shops. A handy number they think, yes anything from A to Z in their books. I hear the voices multiplying, come in and buy food, come in and buy a jumper, come in and buy trousers, come in and buy a jacket, come in and buy wallpaper. Come in and buy a TV set, come in and buy a record player, come in and buy furniture, come in and buy gardening tools, come in and buy a wallet, come in and buy books, come in and say your prayers. He couldn't see the faces but the voices were like fists pounding his ears in, going around and around in circles. The lights twinkling in the street, the shop windows lit up, the window dummies put their hands up to their mouths, laughing at him. The whole town was laughing at him, doors were flung open, people walked up and down the pavements goading him. Goading him, goading him, goading him. They ran indoors and returned with more things, they sat down on the footpaths and twiddled knobs, examining all their things carefully under the street lights. One voice boomed through the crowds, all together now aaaaaaaaaah! They preened in front of the shop windows. The crowds were everywhere, surrounding him, laughing at him, pointing at the things in the shop windows. 'You can't have them, ha! ha!' They hugged and kissed the things they had brought out into the streets. All around him was the mimicking faces. A crowd of men gathered around him. Four of them landed on top of him. They beat him and beat him to pulp. They all cheered. Then a hand grabbed his hair and wrenched his head back. A man bent over him and drew on him in lipstick. He looks better. He looks more cheerful. That's it, smiley, smiley, you sucker. One got his legs, another his shoulders and heaved him into the middle of the street. Wonderful, wonderful fun a voice shouted. More, more, more. They stamped their feet on the ground and yelled at him. They threw him up in the air, higher and higher then fell around laughing. 'Let him go,' a voice said, 'He's dead and done.'

But you couldn't keep my Da down. 'I'll give you somethin' to fuckin' remember me by,' he roared. 'You plopped me down like a lump of shit without so much as a by your leave. A lump of bloody shit, that's what I am.'

He waited, another splutter of steam came out of him, he was up and at it again. 'A fuckin' number dead and done, I'm a bum, I'm a bum, I'm a friggin' bum.'

The terror no longer two fat fingers pinching his neck but waves from the sea drowning him out as he floated like a corpse down the street. I own my job don't I? Don't I own my job? He scratched his balls through the soft cloth of his trousers and then felt them tenderly. He stopped, pressed his big head against the cool pane of a shop window. His big head bursting with cold feverish pain. I own my job don't I? Don't I own my job? But they took it away, they took it away and said, 'A grand day. One of the best yet.'

His blue eyes glinted cruelly in the sunshine. It's my job. No one can take my job away from me. I own my job. Don't I own my job? The shame flooded through him, oh this kip, this godforsaken kip. If only he could think of something, an original idea, he all alone in his little hovel thinking something that was definite, certain, would never budge and roll over on him coming up all eyes and chips of wood that floated away at a touch. He struck at the pain in his head with his fist and sunk down into the footpath. I got to get air, I got to get out. The crowds swelled up around him and came at him again. They tore at him, a vile look on their faces, he felt a shriek gather in his throat, 'You stinkin' rotten bastards.'

But they circled around him, he tried to get to his feet but they knocked him back down. His face smashed into the ground, they fell on him kicking him, beating him up, he crawled out from under thousands of bodies. Legs, hands, eyes, mouths, noses, chewing at their own flesh, at each other, tearing their pricks off, strangling each other, they set fire to the buildings, the flames leaping into the air, burning charred lumps of flesh rolling around the streets. He fell over into legs, breasts, a screaming mass of shrivelled up bodies. The sound of the squad cars behind him, the heifers on the job, they're joining in, they love it, batons crashing down on skulls with the screams scrambling like white mice through the streets. He stumbled up off the footpath with the crowds murdering and hacking at each other, arms rolling over the side of the road, waiting for him to shovel them up. I own my job, don't I own my job? A baton hitting the side of his head, a mixture of spittle and blood drooling down his chin, he scrambled up and over, he didn't stop running until he was outside the town roaring, my blood on that bastard's baton, he waited for his head to clear, he looked around, twenty thousand houses standing side by side stared back at him, all the same size, the same concrete slabs, the front doors all the same colours. A group of men streamed past him.

'How'ya. How'ya. See ya later Joe.'

'You. You. Go to hell,' he choked. A face floated up in front of him, a face, mouth, murmur, 'Go to hell'.

A head moved in closer, the nose dribbling water, he held onto the side of a wall for support. The face stared into his.

'Are you alright?'

'How's it goin' Joe?'

Three foot square, he thought. Hear it pounding in me skull, relentless pounding in me skull, let me in, let me in, no light, light all gone now, no movement from below, sound coming from mouth, dry mouth, all is three foot square, no air, no air, all three foot square, all of it.

He reared his head up, sniffing, smelling the sound, the words, 'Are you alright Joe? How'ya.' Sounds with no smells, no touch, words that couldn't be embraced, beaten, kicked or seen. He didn't want to talk ever again. Never, never open his mouth and speak his mind out. Talking did no good, they all agreed with you that you were getting a raw deal, they all agreed and walked away. And there he was left with his own raw deal stuck in his craw. No one was going to do anything for him anymore. No one was going to bargain for his labour anymore. He had nothing to sell now. Nothing at all to sell.

My Ma had sensed the change in him. The brute force in his face was now visible, he didn't bother to hide it for there was nothing to hold him down anymore. The power of it filling her with envy as she watched it, circling carefully around him doing nothing to restrain him, but careful not to give him an excuse to point it her way. She was an experienced manouverer in evading him, knowing how to ghost walk, ghost talk and disappear when the brute force was out of control. Later she would tell the women what a bastard he was but for now she was trapped in the magic of it – You can force people to do what you want if you've got the muscle.

Da read the evening paper cover to cover and called out to Ma, 'Will ya listen to this,' he said. Then he'd point a finger at her to grab her attention again and say, 'Will ya, will ya, my God almighty who do they think they're coddin.' It turned his stomach to see the nonsense that went on about killing.

'No one more shocked then me,' says the minister about a particular killing. And then if it isn't the priest's turn, 'no one more shocked then me either,' as if they were out playing ball in the schoolyard. They'll outshock each other in quare style one of these days. That's what happens when they cut the balls off you, buy you off with the regular few bob and the bonus and what have you got but a pink-faced arse-licker in a pin stripe suit and a case under his arm the size of a postage stamp. God give me patience, he blessed himself and shook his head in disbelief to emphasise what hypocrites they were. His bitterness made him look ugly and as his viciousness grew to the size of a football inside him she became quieter withdrawing gracefully into a shell covered in large diamonds and opals. One tear lay on her cheek frozen and perfectly-shaped while her pale hand lay on her heart in place of the withered tulip he'd given her on their wedding day. She sat quietly waiting on him to finish the paper so she could have a read of it.

'God's curse but the government are goin' all out to do somethin' about things,' he said. 'Only thing is all the schemes are for young people.'

'Is that right?' she asked.

'That's right. They think when you're not working you'll go 'way and do them a favour.'

'Is that right,' she asked.

'That's right. They think you'll stop breathin' altogether.' And they are not the only ones, he thought, hiding his face behind the paper. Am I the fool not to know all these long years the looks on their faces, the ways and means of getting rid of you and tee-heeing when they think you're not looking. A man never forgets his enemies especially when they sleep under his own roof night after night. Am I a fool? he pondered. No I am not. Am I to be taken lightly? No I am not.

Fodder, fodder, dying away moaaaaaaaaaning son, son, my cherry red twisting around inside your old grey coat, fodder, fodder, who art in heaven. Out of the corner of his mouth he whistled and it came out all gargled like waiting for Jesus to blow his nose on his sleeve and say, 'Ukk the oxen, Ukk the oxen.' Jesus was a ruby red on the Bishop's finger but the Bishop didn't sing plodding along the road to the gallows with your ankles tied.

I want to be a good boy and do all the right things, I really do. Ma said I had it in me but *he* wasn't so sure about me. I think it's a big gamble as to how I'll turn out in the end. Another time she said it was all up to me – as if I had something to do with it. The only thing is I'm oozing with charm and everyone loves me for it. Charm and good looks, I'm short on good looks but you can't have everything. I wonder why I can't have everything and why some people have more then others. It's as if God isn't fair just like Ma and Da when they have a row and turn the house into a counting house: One for you and one for me. And then world war breaks out because they can't agree to share things.

'I should get a bit extra,' Da, says. 'I'm a man.' And he flexes his old rubbery muscles like wellington boots across the room at her so she can see he's king pin. And then she starts totting up all the years of her life and all she did for us and she looks down her nose at him and says, triumphantly, 'So what? I'm a mother.'

He watched her get up and clear the things off the table restless as a billygoat toing and froing across the floor nonstop.

'Tryin' to outdo the rest of the world, eh! Tryin' to pip us at the post, eh! For Christ's sake slow down.' But there she was up and down, in and out, up and down, and as if he's not bad enough he's got a lump on the side of his neck.

'Did you hear me,' he shouted. 'I have a lump.'

'What kind of lump?' she asked demurely, drawing herself up to her full size and sniffing distastefully across at him.

'What does it matter what kind? It's a lump,' he shouted, thinking, there's love and caring for you now with a look on her face like she was someone's lost shoe.

He might be dying, she thought. What will I do if he's dying? How will I go on? I can't go on. She chewed her bottom lip wishing she was a baby in her mother's arms. Her mother rocking her back and forth and singing to her, 'It's all right love. It's all right.'

A dreamy faraway look was in her eyes and he shook his head and shivered with fear. And then he laughed it away, telling himself it was a boil that would go away with itself when it was good and ready. She went off again to rummage around for some rubbish or other and not a pick on her and no wonder. Now he was on the dole he could keep a good eye on things around the house and rest easy knowing there would be no change from one end of the day to another. That's all a man asks for, let things be, no change whatsoever, he prays to God, but nothing will do the young people but that they throw everything out and have nothing left at the end of the day. Bloody good enough for them as long as I don't come into it, he thought. He read the papers for the killings and he knew one thing fair and square, the papers didn't know everything. There was one killing that never hit the light of day until months after it was done.

After a while he went down the garden to give himself a break from the monotony of the house.

'Joe,' she cooed down the garden after him.

'Yea,' he cooed back.

'What are you doin' down there?' she cooed.

'Eh.'

'Come on what is it.'

'I can't hear you.'

She threw the window wide open. 'Now can you hear me?' she called down.

'I 'spect so.' He teased her.

'You expect so. You can hear me, Joe. I know you can.'

'If you say so,' he teased her again.

He was crafty as a ferret, she couldn't get him to respond with softness and she never thought of licking him (all over) like I did to make him laugh. If you tickled his fancy he'd do anything for you.

'The wheelbarrow's gone,' she called down. 'Joe?'

'What?'

'Did you hear what I said?'

'Yea.'

'Its stolen, Joe.'

'Arrea I loaned it out.'

'To who? They didn't give it back.'

'They forgot.'

'You're an awful man loanin' things out.'

He rolled the sleeve of his shirt up to his elbows and with the soft blue wrinkled folds of cotton wiped his running nose. He went back to the digging, upturning the sods of grass with slow regular movements. He worked on, his back aching and the sweat gathering and rolling down his face. He rubbed his forehead with the back of his hand and stood up straight to relieve the ache in the lower part of his back. He dug our garden as if he was shovelling a tunnel into the bowels of the earth so he could have a direct line to hell.

'Joe, you'll have a heart attack the way you're carrying on,' she called down the garden to him. 'For God's sake stop. Come up and have a cup of tea.'

He turned around at this fuss. Pleased she was taking notice of him, he went back happily to the digging. But every so often he'd stand up dead straight and roar at the world. 'It's all a load of balls.'

That's when I heard the lion roar in him and I could see for myself Da was as wild a beast as you could ever hope to capture. Ever after I listened out for the low growls and the tetchy snapping howls and at the tea table I suddenly burst out into an old pop song, 'In the jungle, the mighty jungle the lion sleeps tonight'. He eyed me lazily across the table and I swear he winked not friendly-like but 'Watch it pal or I'll eat you up for supper'. My knife slipped on the side of my plate and I smiled slyly at the clink of it. You should never cage a lion up and if you do, make sure you are on the outside.

'Eat up like a good boy,' Ma said.

Even though I was fourteen she was still pretending I was only seven years old. I think she wanted that year to be forever and ever because a lot of exciting things must have happened.

That was the year I said, 'She's the one for me.'

'It's all a load of balls,' he roared up our back garden again in case she missed the first roar. She straightened up instantly and flexed her ears like a fox listening intently for any signs of danger. She stood trance-like, dizzy with fear because danger was all around, as every fox knows lions have no mercy for them. But he was only exercising his tonsils that day. She sighed wishing she was a widow drawing a pension and lording it over everyone else for a change. She balanced delicately on tiptoe so she could get a better look at him through the window. As she returned to her cleaning she sighed, she was left with a right bastard on her hands. She must have forgotten she loved him from that time on? Or was it all because she loved him?

Temptation got the better of her again and she went back to the open window to talk down to him.

'Joe,' she called. 'You remember the day I bought the lace tablecloth.'

'Oh sure,' he said. 'When was it? 1956. I remember the day well.'

'It was just after we were married.'

'Thanks for reminding me.'

'I never used it. I put it by for a special occasion.'

'I'll never get this done if you don't shut up.'

'That tablecloth reminds me of long ago,' she said folding her arms and leaning up against the window as if she was all set for a good chat. 'Does anything remind you of long ago?'

'I remember nothin'. Now will you let me get on with it.'

'Everyone has memories, even you.'

'Leave me be.' He shouted up the garden.

'There isn't a human being born hasn't got memories. It's impossible not to have them,' she said.

'Well I'm the living proof of the impossible.'

He leaned on the shovel, took a hankey from his back pocket to wipe his forehead again. Digging was no picnic after all especially now as he was so unfit. But he rose like a king and the stately robes fell in soft folds around his feet. King, king, king, come to the palace and meet the queen.

'For God's sake woman leave me alone,' he said. 'Can't you see I'm puffed out.'

You see Ma was doomed from the start without hope or a chance until she met Da and when she married him she swore to love honour and obey him until the day she died. And even when he was in the slammer she told all the neighbours he was working away and living in digs for a while. Sometimes she boasted to the other women saying, 'Actually he's staying in a hotel.' And he sent her a note instructing her to cut out any bits about him in the evening paper and to make up a scrap book for him. He puzzled my Ma like the pieces of a jigsaw she couldn't put together.

'I don't understand that man,' she'd sigh. 'I can't make head nor tail of him,' and her face would wrinkle up into puzzled creases and a halo of yellow appeared around her head.

'I know nothin',' I said.

'What love?'

'I know nothin',' I said. 'I know that one.'

'What are you talkin' about?' She got huffy whenever I said something that made her uneasy. Oh what did I say? Oh her heart was broken long, long ago and she said to herself, 'No one will ever get in near me. No one.' She couldn't remember anything specific that broke her heart and it was so ordinary to have it broken little by little.

She came around and sat up on the sill. She swung her heels against the wall like a little girl and he watched out of the corner of his eye hiding his adoration in a gruff moan.

'What are you doin', you'll break the bloody sill on me,' he moaned, fearing the collapse of his house as well as himself.

'Break the sill! How can I break the sill, it's made of concrete. All sills are made from concrete,' she said sarcastically.

'Did I ask you for a speech, did I? Get out of the window, get down off it. You'll break it on me.'

They fenced around some more until they were satisfied that they were still hale and hearty and could screw each other into kingdom come if they wanted to. Finally he came in scraping the soles of his boots against the lip of the top step then he stamped down hard on the mat before going into the kitchen. She had the tea all ready and waiting for him. She took two cups and saucers down from the press and as she opened the drawer where the spoons were kept she realised she'd taken two of the good cups and saucers down. She put them back in the press and replaced them with old ones because he'd let her down badly.

She kept her back to him as he stretched out in the chair

gazing out the window. The passion rose and fell in our kitchen like a limping leprechaun on its way to the barber's for a crewcut. Sometimes they were tempted to have a good time and to hell with God, his secret ledgers and his impeccable memory, but my Ma and Da were brave strong people and they withstood all temptations to have a good time because it was only for having children and they were determined to get to heaven.

Ma pinned all her dreams on me like a badge of honour now that he had let her down. With my new status in mind I named myself the first prince charming in our family. But she still remained gloomy and Da thought I was a hopeless case because I never give an opinion on anything until I see how the land lies first. I am only a little prince and though I'm fourteen years old my voice hasn't broken yet.

'Your head's full of cotton wool,' Ma complained.

'And you're sly,' Da added.

But they can't see I'm storing everything away in my mind like the squirrel with his nuts. Da throws his arms up in the air like a boxer in the ring and says, 'I give up. I can't get through to you.' I make them so unhappy and they frown and spout and wriggle about in their chairs and get tense. Da slaps the newspaper over to the next page as if he'd love to rip it apart. And she closes her eyes and turns away from me with her I'm-not-speaking-to-you look. And she smokes like a chimney pot on fire. I make them unhappy as if I'm full of a dark dangerous power and they fear me. I watch with wonder at their distress and if I sing aloud like I want to they'll probably kill themselves, so I turn on my heels with his voice in my ear.

'He doesn't say a bloody word. We're not good enough for him now.'

I examine my face in the mirror trying to see the power in me. Trying to feel it and touch it with my hands. Trying to know it so I can make it work wonders for me. My face isn't the same as it was yesterday. Every day I look a bit different as if something is taking me over. I turn my head to one side to have a look at my profile. I can't see what is happening to me. I can't catch it and yet my face is changing. I get plainer by the day. I hope I don't lose my charm or I'm bunched.

When Da told her he couldn't even get the odd job anymore she nearly broke down and gave into his need for comfort. Normally it was against her principles to comfort an ignorant brute of a man but her arms flew up and opened to receive him and Da felt the rush of crying inside him, the crying that would bring him to his knees in front of her and then he'd feel lower then her. And then where are you? Instead he spoke gruffly.

'Ah well, something else will turn up.'

'Sure it will. It always does.'

'Anyway I'm not upset. I couldn't give a curse about it.'

'Course you're not.'

'I'm off out,' he said.

'Will you be late?' She spoke casually as if it was no matter one way or another to her.

'Don't wait up,' he said.

Instinct rose like the bristle of hair on the back of the fox's neck. The lion was pacing his cage, his face a kindly smile on it yet she felt he was forcing it, that he was watching her carefully, hoping she'd fall into a trap and give him another excuse to beat her. She held on, careful not to snap but to outwit him and leave him with no excuse, so he wouldn't be able to use her to relieve himself. She said nothing, instead she lowered her head modestly like a handmaiden and gazed at the pattern of the lino on the floor. Inside she was weeping for the good old days when money wasn't as important as people but it was such a long, long time ago.

My Ma is a natural bloodsucker, she even has had the blood sucked out of herself. One time the doctor put her on tablets and told her she was anaemic and I ran down the path after him and said before I disappeared up into a puff of smoke: 'Dracula. After midnight watch out, my Mam is a bitch for blood.' Her teeth grew long and sharp shortly after tea. You could see the need rising in her and her long thin bony face becoming grey and strained-looking.

'You should drink stout,' Da told her. 'It'd build you up.'

But she didn't want stout, she wanted my blood, see, for strength. And my bloom for roses in her hair. And she wanted a sheen to her skin like I had because I reminded her of strawberry beds.

'Watch out, here she comes,' I howled loudly and my Mam said 'What is it? What's the matter?'

'I've a pain right here,' I said pointing to my belly.

'You ate too quick,' she said, 'it's indigestion.'

'No,' I moaned, 'It's something else.'

It was far better to be sick than sorry in our house.

Ma became famous when she was young for being a bitch. It was one of her thrones, her sacred rites. Well she wouldn't do you a favour if she could. And she always insisted on doing you one when you didn't need it. Everything that was against life she was in favour of. The right to slander the good name of life itself, the tenacity and endurance and determination needed to spit on life morning, noon and night. The energy she had given to fighting life, she told me. The spite and bitterness and maliciousness she'd spread among the women on the road. She'd sapped other women's spirits, depressed them with bad news, gossiped about intimate secrets she'd sworn on the Bible to keep her mouth shut about. 'Life is terrible Mrs O'Brien. Terrible. Well I'm off to get the messages before he gets home in front of me.' She spread misery as far and wide as she could, 'I destroyed four good characters this morning. Whew, what a marvellous day, I'm worn out wrecking. I'm a bitch. I'm a bitch, big bite bitch, you can't take that away from me.'

'Hate, hate with all your might,' my Gran told her. 'Hate, hate with every breath in your body, hate till you fall dead to the ground. Hate till you can hate no more. D'ya hear me now?' Gran shouted, hate, hate, like a war cry.

'You'll never be free unless you hate,' Gran said. 'Hate's the first step to freedom, girlie.' Gran's nostrils flared out like a horse's as she sniffed out the enemy and jabbed a finger at them. 'That way. This way. Turn to the left. To the left I said dope.'

There was no hate left in Gran when she died. Her body collapsed like a sack of potatoes. Her knees hunched up to her belly, and her arms fell like twigs by her side. There was only her old eyes with the hate flowing free and pure through them. That was the way she emptied the inside of herself out into the world when she couldn't get out of bed.

'I've done me bit,' she whispered proudly. And then she snuffed it.

When she was older Ma became famous for her headaches – 'I can't I've got a headache.' It was like her autograph, in a circumference of seven miles everybody knew that Ma didn't climb mountains or swim the seven seas, she got headaches instead. When she was a young girl a headache caught Gran's attention far quicker than a laugh or a scream. Gran had seven of them to look after, four boys and three girls and they all laughed and screamed, but they didn't get headaches.

'She's delicate,' Gran said. She liked it, it sounded like the eyes of the gentle doe from the forest of her dreams. Colds, flus, wheezy chests all erupted throughout the winter in her thin body. 'She's the delicate one all right.'

And later it came in handy for keeping the boys off her. How could you jump someone so wan and doe-like? No it was healthy women that got jumped on the way home from the dances in the nearby hall.

'A bad eater?' Another woman looked down at her and sympathised.

'Don't be talkin',' Gran said. 'She won't touch a spoon of food for me.'

'Ah God bless her, she's out on her own aren't you love?'

Ma fought her way to fame with the sword of a thousand headaches. She was a delicate titbit that could be nibbled at but not pounced on. Pouncing was vulgar, it lacked style and reeked of bad breeding. Bad breeding was one of her hates. For instance clod-hoppers from the surrounding countryside who were all O's and A's buck teeth and big feet country boys who didn't know how to treat a lady. And boys training to be thieves more than likely give you a stolen bracelet as a birthday present. Street fighting boys in training to beat people up before stealing from them. Ma fought them with fine gestures, a flick of her slim wrists at the right moment, the turn of her head just as they'd start wolf whistling, the scent of perfume to remind them that they were dealing with a real lady. The shine of her hair was a mirror to blind their eyes with. And she used the rippling movements of her long hair to slap them across the face for thinking crude thoughts about her as she passed by. And she was never on time for a date so the boy would know how popular she was and how lucky to have the time to give him at all.

But what about a shining example? A shining example woman married for true love, and there was a memory of one at least in most families. Gran said that their shining example was a big fat woman with round padded arms, a belly the size of three wash basins and a wholesome honest face. Biddy, big fat shining example woman was passed like a gold casket from mind to mind, 'Don't forget what Biddy done. Our Biddy was one of the best. Biddy was a hero, did you know that? Did I tell you that before? From mind to mind, what a woman, you could cry for a week in her arms and she'd stay with you. You'd be a poor love, instead of a bloody nuisance, with Biddy around. And Biddy did it for love, could you credit that. A lovely woman, couldn't find lovelier than Biddy. So sweet-natured, nature like a fresh plum, Biddy had. All the babies that came out of Biddy were loved and cared for equally. She thrived and blossomed on each birth. Then one woman thought we can't keep calling her Biddy like this, we'll put a little something in front of her name, for Biddy was a deserving cause, they said. That dear sweet woman why she's the makings of a saint, they began to murmur amongst themselves. And "Biddy was a saint", was the thought that was transferred to the mind of the next woman.'

'One of your mothers was a saint.' Gran crooned. 'Saint Biddy, a darling body.'

'Biddy was an apple blossom?' Ma asked running into Gran. 'Was that it?'

Gran twisted her ear for her, 'A saint I told you. She was a saint.'

And when Ma got a headache, the ache made her bunch up inside herself even more than usual and totally confused with which memory was Biddy and which the woman before her – she said, 'Biddy was a bitch then, what?'

'A saint, a bloody saint.' Gran roared. 'I'm sick telling you, a saint is a saint is a saint.'

Every evening Da would think, What will I do with meself tonight. He'd thought the same thought for years and always the answer was, I don't know, or, we'll see. A way out was to call in on someone or hope someone called in on him for to sit staring at Ma for the night only made his blood boil. In the beginning he stayed in and ignored her completely. He read the paper, watched the television, but always her face would burst through the paper on him or appear on the screen of the television, 'Come 'ere, bark,' with a sneer that would make a weaker man cut her up for supper. And every time he opened his mouth to speak the wrong thing came out of it. One sentence led to another and before he knew where he was he was saying things he never meant to say. Then the frustrated silence until the only thing left was in reaching for his hat and coat and out onto the street.

'Come eight o'clock I set off out onto the road,' Da said. 'I walked through the town, down main street and a mile on I headed straight for the woods. I have seven good spots picked out for the seven days of the week and there I stay for the night in the company of a bottle I keep stashed in my coat pocket. This is the place to be away from human company and the barking of dogs. But somewhere around me, out there in the darkness a boy and girl are coming my way thinking they're alone and they can do what they like. It takes you days, weeks, even months to hunt them down, when you go one end of the woods they're up the other end and by the time you get to them they've heard you and it's no bloody use. It puts me in a foul mood to see a night wasted like that when all they have to do is come my way to take away the agony. It's only the squeaking of strangers that can relieve the grieving, I'm down to that. They don't like being caught at it and they like it less when they see my pecker waving at them well a pity about them. Once a month touch wood I come across a couple lying on top of each other, it's the best time to catch them, they freeze all the better and scream all the louder for you. You can do anything in this world so long as the other party is already feeling guilty. You can buy silence without having to put your hand in your back pocket. Everyone has a secret and you don't even have to know what that secret is, that's the cod of it. Young people think they invented wife swapping and loose living – God bless them hasn't man been shooting his load since Noah's Ark for Christ's sake? And has man been particular who it's with? Never. One man for one woman and they've got you exactly where they want you. Anyway the nights are long and I indulge in a bit of harmless fun, keeping company you might say while I still can. In my heyday I use to frighten the shit out of the children coming home from school. They use to come up to the woods here to collect conkers and nuts and lo and behold who was here waiting for them with his pecker on the ready. I believe they grew fond of me. From four to eight years old is the ideal age for the human race in general. We're at our peak at that age. We've hit the heights.

The woman tries to get me to go to mass of a Sunday morning. Bad sess to it there's nothing worse than seeing them hareing off to the masses as if it mattered a tuppenny damn to them whether he was or he wasn't. It's a consolation that's all it is. And you can't get past the front porch without putting your hand in your back pocket. I can't be bothered going for the sake of the neighbours either.

'I'll grieve at home thank you, it's cheaper', I said to her. 'And the lie in does me good.'

'Grieve?'

'Aye.'

'Grieve about what?'

'I don't know, do I?'

She nods her head in that way of hers as if I'm a hopeless case and off she goes on her own to examine the scarves and hats and the cut of the coats for the morning. She comes back tanked up with enough gossip to keep her going for the rest of the week. A marriage breaking up, this one running away. A long sickness can keep her dewy-eyed for hours. There's nothing brings on the yawns more then hearing that things are going right for someone. They all go to mass and take an interest in religion, including my sons. I am the only sane one left here, the rest have long since been bought off lock, stock and barrel. A splash of water on their foreheads and they're booking their flights to heaven. A blessing from the priest and they're sitting on God's lap in their best bib and tucker. God give me patience.

The woman couldn't leave well enough alone. One evening she hounded me after the dinner about it. 'Am I to take it you don't believe? You're one of those atheists. Am I to take it?'

'Take what you like from it,' I said.

'People are asking questions about you,' she said.

'Then tell them the truth.'

'What is the truth? What am I to tell them?'

'Tell them it's sweet fuck-all to me.'

My sons. They are coming for me soon. Dick and Andy have a job on the building sites in England. They bed and board and come home the odd year. In between they send a letter. *Dear Da the work is going well. The food's alright. How are you and Mam, take care of yourselves.* If anything has meaning for me in this world it's my sons. Big strong boys with thick shining heads of hair and fine shaped feet fit to dip in a soup bowl. And the sort of work they do brings a fine colour to their skins all year round. I myself am a fine gardener when I put my mind to it. It's the ideal job, fresh air, come and go as you please, nothing too permanent about it. When the money is short in the big houses the gardener's the first to go. I like the variety and the feeling you can walk out any time you like, there's always another big house just around the corner. At least there was, now every old arse-lick in the country is going house to house looking for work. It's not simple anymore, I'm blocked at every turn.

I never liked working. There's too much giving orders and treating you like a dog with the mange. I like to wake up when I wake up and not on someone else's say so. I like to eat when I'm hungry, instead of come one o'clock you have to order yourself to be starving. It's the sure road to lunacy. The woman doesn't understand the conditions of work not having done a tap since she said, 'I do'. But now it's worse, now I don't even have the chance of saying no. The irony is that by a stroke of fate I'm become a yes-man. There's nothing the big boys would like to hear more than that. Caught in the trap after thirty years of giving them the slip, my lips are sealed. To tell the truth if she pulled herself together and went out instead of me you wouldn't hear a murmur out of me. Life is too distracting to concentrate on any one thing for longer then thirty seconds flat.

I liked it in the woods. I felt at home. When I was there I loved all things and when I went back out onto the road I hated all things. There's no accounting for taste. I see myself as a chaperone. I am never idle. I make haste when I have to and I've patience to burn if it's necessary. I feel it's my calling, even say when I have the sniffles or my back is aching I will turn up here at the latest 8.30. But that's only the night shift. The day shift, well by the time I have breakfast and train her in some more, it's eleven o'clock. I usually take a couple of sandwiches with me and a flask of tea. From then until six I'm waiting in the woods. It's a miracle that industry kept going for as long as it did. The amount of people that disappear during the hours of two to four for a quick fuck must be close to the million mark. They don't all come here thank God, a man only has one pecker and two hands.

The children come after school with school bags on their backs, they come here because they've a lot to hide. Once they get use to me they bring their friends along for a peek of my pecker. Their faces light up with excitement when they see me.

I'm very discreet. I usually slip out from behind a tree with my feast unzipped, give them a roasting with my tongue and off I go. All too often it's a whinge instead of a good healthy scream. And then I suppose they go on home to their tea. But you'd be surprised at how discreet they are, never a word about me to whoever looks after them. I look upon myself as a social worker. The first time I came here, shortly after I was married, industry was really only coming into its own. New factories were springing up every year and whereas before I could walk one end of the town to the other at my usual speed, it became impossible with this new breed that arrived. They were not fighting men, they believed in using their brains instead, God help us. The ideal time for using your brains is between the age of one to four. After that it's only a matter of following orders. I never liked the new breed of man. I yearn for the sort of man who will put his life on the line when it's necessary. A smart-arse will never do that. What will happen to them all as they sift through the ruins of industry and blame each other? No one is to blame, we are all innocent as babes in arms. If only they could see that they'd have a night's sleep for a change. As it is no one sleeps.

I don't know what's going on from one end of the day to the next. I'm not the only one. I don't say this to console myself but as a fact that must be faced. No one knows what's going on. No one knows what they are doing. And we are not allowed sleep. It's a sad state of affairs. Is this why I grieve? I doubt it. I don't give a curse whether they sink or swim as long as I'm not in it. One evening a woman arrived here alone. This was so unusual that I hesitated to let her feast her eyes on my pecker. I stayed behind a tree and made my way slowly around it, keeping my back against the bark of the tree. She seemed to be looking for something in the bushes. She was so absorbed in poking through the bushes that I became just as absorbed and concerned that she find what she was looking for. I suppose for a few short seconds I fell in love. Eventually she went away and I returned to my spot for the night my pecker unloved. But I was well-prepared for the next one. Falling in love is the worst disease to befall man since life began. The best time to fall in love is between the ages of ninety and ninety-five.

Are you about your father's business? Are you about your mother's business? Are you about your own business? These are the burning questions of the day. And what about your uncle's and your aunt's? Whose business are you about and between the hours of what, say twenty-four hours in the day, how many of these are devoted to their business? Are you about your country's business? Are you about the business of your parish priest? And what about the doctor, which reminds me I have a lump. Are you about his business? The discussion of ailments can take up a fair proportion of anyone's day. Falling in love at the ripe old age of ninety is what justice is all about, by then it won't matter a shite to you.

I sometimes wonder what I was doing sitting in the woods night after night. Let it piss rain and there I was faithful as ever sitting on the bark of a tree with my coat over my head. I was waiting for my turn. That's it. One day it would be my turn and I would go no more to the woods. I would probably grieve a while as I am prone to doing but then I would go on to my turn and try to be cheerful about it. I have never smiled or laughed or told anyone a joke. Never. It simply hasn't come up yet. I'm not sure how many people laugh in this world. I would love to know how many do and what they are laughing at. Is it me? In all probability I'm keeping a fair proportion of the human race amused just by being here. I'm not useless then thanks be to God. I have met people who are completely useless and they still insist on living. I'm full of admiration for hopeless cases. I love them. They must go on if only for the sake of cheering at the end of it all. The hopeless cases generally rule the world. People are kind, the minute you say you are useless they stick a crozier in your hand and call you a bishop or put you into a large room with a handful of papers and call you a president. There is no end to their kindness. They don't want you to despair. I will go as far as to say they insist on it. This is what the lavish banquets are all about. They waltz until the early hours of the morning and then they come out onto balconies specially built for them and wave to all the kind people of the world. I intend to despair of everything until the day I die.

The thought of loving another human being makes me vomit. I am completely against it. There is too much of it going on all over the world. It's bad for you. It wouldn't surprise me to find out that it is the root cause of my lump. My family loved me and all my relations. I am easy to love. Right from the beginning I was my mother's pride and joy. I came from a large family. There is too much love in large families. They were all at it. We were all fairly easy going. There was no big push on to do this or that, not like nowadays. You could do nothing and they would still love you. It's enough to make any man sick. I got so much of it that if anyone had the neck to love me now I would laugh at them. That's it. That is what would make me laugh. I try not to love people, but everyone knows I am warm-hearted. They say they can always rely on me to do them a good turn. The woman doesn't understand that some people need money more then we do. They come begging to me to help them out with a few bob. A man can't refuse his friends. A man can't turn his back on his comrades. I see myself as a socialist. I believe there should be an even spread of money to begin with. Then we'll see where we go from there. I have lived life according to my beliefs. If there is an extra pound in my pocket and a friend is in need I'll give it to him. He in his turn will do it for me. There are a lot of backstreet socialists only waiting for the call to arms. You wait and see, one day the smart-arses will be overthrown. The meek will inherit the earth, it says so in the Bible. The Bible is tripe. Everyone knows about it but nobody reads it. It's the same with all so-called good books. The boy reads too much. It's bad for him. On his death bed he will recall all the tripe he's read and regret it. I don't like him. I have never liked him. He's not my sort of boy. His head is in the clouds. He is not a socialist. I can tell by him that he's always in love. It's a way of life with him. He thinks he is on the right track. One day he will be a smart-arse. He will come to me and say father socialism is not the answer. That will be the day he becomes a fully grown man. He will have the answer to the system. He will feel he can beat it. He will feel his vision is the one the world is waiting on. He will ride roughshod over his father just to prove he is a man. How can I like him?

Dick and Andy are different. They are coming for me soon. They understand the principles of equality. They understand it is wrong that one man butter his bread while the other man has no bread to butter. They understand we must stick together. I don't know where the boy came from. He's my son and yet he's not my son. There is a black sheep in every family. I must forgive him. I can't forgive him. I'll think about it after the lump is removed. What did I say that for? Why am I thinking that? Surely it is a boil like all other boils. There is no top on it that's what worries me. Is it a new kind of boil? A new boil for a new age. I am turning into a new man. In spite of everything they are changing me. I cling to the past because there is no present. People talk about the present as if there is something happening. There is nothing happening. It's the same as it's always been. The past is the present. If I were to describe one day in my life, I'd be describing all the days of my life. The woman has been there from day one. Of course there are minor changes but they are not worth bothering about. I saw her as a young woman, I saw her as an old woman and then I saw her as a young woman again. I even went to her funeral once. Now she is middle-aged. The future I know nothing about except that one day it will be the past too. I see myself as a fearless man. The woman is frightened. Every day of her life she is frightened. There is nothing to be frightened about, try telling that to her. The habits of a lifetime make no difference to her. She is not consoled. She says it's alright for me. She doesn't say how, just that it is. She is weak. All women are weak. They are all frightened. I've trained her to do as she is told. I give her money. I give her food and shelter. She wants for nothing. In spite of all my efforts she's still frightened. I don't understand women. I don't want to understand them, I'm quite clear on that. It's bad for me. I don't like them. I've never liked them. I'll never change my mind on that score. Still I've done my best for her. It's not enough. It's never enough.

The boy on turning the corner sneaked a look at me over his shoulder. His hair flowed well down past his shoulders, the colour of a raven's it was. He had a silver earring in one ear and a red scarf dotted with small black flowers tied loosely around his neck. He lived in one of the houses in Grattan Lane. He was two classes ahead of me in school, that made him around sixteen. I'd been watching him for weeks. Ever so casually his coal black eyes took me in from head to toe with a smouldering come-and-get-me look. He hurried on around the corner, down Lexington Street and took up his position on Rahineys' corner. Most days he stood there between two and four. When he'd get fed up he'd take off for a short walk and return again. My spot was on the main street about one hundred yards up on the opposite side of the road to his. I knew by him that he was a professional nicker, and I hoped I didn't look like a beginner to him. I tried to look suave and easy going as I stood in the doorway, I whistled a tune by Frank Sinatra, *I'll do it my way*. I love old songs best. I watched him standing on his patch while all around him there was a soft glowing light like the kind of light you see of a late summer's evening. He was aglow with love. We kept our eye on one another for a few weeks and then one day he crossed the street and came up to talk to me.

'Howya?' he said.

'Howya?' I said.

'I seen ya around,' he said.

I nodded.

'You goin' back to school next year?' he asked.

'Yeah,' I said. 'I've another two years to do.'

'I'm finished,' he said. He took a packet of cigarettes out from the inside pocket of his jacket and offered me one.

'What do ya think of the band, what do ya call them, the Saturns?'

'They're great,' I said.

'They're rubbish.'

'Are they?'

'The best band of the lot is Magic. You play yourself?'

'No. Do you?'

'I play the guitar a lot. I'm hopin' to start up a band soon. Me and Karl Mullens. D'ya know Karl Mullens?'

'Yeah.'

'Do ya?'

'No.'

'D'ya know him to see? He's a tall fellow with fair hair. He's a great bass player.'

'Blonde?'

'Huh?'

'Blonde hair?'

'That's what I said, fair hair.'

'Where do you play?'

'We're gettin' everything together first. We're on the look out for someone to manage us. You get nowhere without a good manager. They just milk you.'

'Do they? There's just the two of you in the band then?'

'We're lookin' for a singer.'

'A singer –'

'Yeah that's what I said a singer.'

'I'm a singer.'

'You are?'

'Sure I am.'

'Lots of fellows can sing of course. You ever think of joinin' a band?'

'No.'

'Well listen if you're interested we're rehearsin' at my house Thursday night. You free Thursday night?'

'I think so.'

'Well listen I live down Grattan Lane. You know it?'

'Yeah.'

'It's number eleven. Thursday night at eight. Right?'

'Right,' I said.

He looked me over and grinned. 'Well, see you then.'

'Yeah, see you.'

To celebrate I went into the supermarket at the top of the main street and nicked some frozen peas, a packet of cold meat and a packet of fish from the freezer. All the way home I kept thinking of how he glowed like a light with love. You don't often see that around. I think you have to believe in love before it shows on your face. I felt so proud he had asked me around to his house. He had a long narrow back and his jeans were skin tight on him. I could see his bum moving up and down like two lovely plums as he went back to his spot. I stayed on another half hour and when I was going he gave me a big wave.

'A present for you,' I said putting the goodies on the table.

'Ah good lad I don't know what I'd do without you.' She came over and gave me a big sloppy kiss on my forehead.

'Ah leave off,' I said.

'Go on,' she said, 'It's true, where would I be without you.' She put the peas and meat in the fridge and kept the packet of fish out for dinner.

'Where's Daddy?' I said.

'He's out.'

'Out where?'

'Ask no questions get no lies,' she purred. 'Who cares about Daddy when I have my own little boy around me? Now get some cooking oil out of the press for me will you love? And some potatoes while you're at it. Two for your Daddy and one for us. He doesn't deserve it of course . . . Where did you go?'

'Just went into town.'

'What did you do?'

'Nothin'.'

'What do you mean nothin'.'

'I did nothin'.'

She turned around too quickly and hit her hip off the edge of the cooker.

'Oh the cooker's moved,' she said and then she did a surprising thing instead of giving out about it she giggled, saying, 'Oh dear me, look what I've done now.'

'Is something the matter?'

'What could be the matter.' She straightened up and shook herself crisp as a new pound note. 'Put the salt and pepper on the table, go and make yourself useful. Go on don't stare at me like that.'

She went quiet and careful, walking across the floor as if she was on a tightrope and she went all sniffy as if the world wasn't good enough for her and she didn't know how she put up with it. I thought she was going to cry but she didn't. I felt relieved because what would I say if she started crying? I'd have gone upstairs and left her to it. She sat down moving the fish fingers about the plate with the fork. I felt as if we had had a great row only I had somehow missed it. When did it happen? What was it about? I had hurt her so much that she couldn't even eat. What was it about me that could do that to her?

'Mam.'

'Hmmm. Yes dear.' She smiled as if the great row was behind us and we were off to a fresh start again.

'I wish Dick and Andy would come home,' I said.

'There's nothin' for them here,' she said.

She spread her hands out over the table to hush the waiting crowds: 'Ladies and gentlemen we are gathered here today to quell the rising of the moon, that glowing vegetable upon whom we heap our lamentations, our procrastinations with the dawn chorus that makes us pray for a world without miracle, for let me tell you, though we swear hand on heart, cap off head, we are but one whisker away from sighting another of those unthinkable, unspeakable sensations that causes the heart to leap about in its trough and sing like a bird nesting innocently in the hangman's knot, in truth we are repulsed by the very thought for it will blind us forever more and leave us as gutted fish with the agony of ecstasy, a crown of thorns, our very own thistledown for what is a miracle but the matter of magnetized reflection, the zinc and the iodine, the rook squatting on its roots, peeing a white fine powder into the bowels of the earth from dawn until dusk!'

The crowds roared for more and she quietened them down with a nicotine-stained finger to her lips and an outstretched hand to cup their cries and store them safely away for another day.

'Is my voice going?' she asked.

'It's good as ever,' I said.

'It sounds a bit hoarse to me.'

'It's grand, Mam'.

'It's strained, a bit tight don't you think?'

'No it's not.'

'Ah sure, where would I be without you. Bring me a glass of water till I gargle. I might be coming down with a sore throat.' She continued on. 'I've seen the headless body of God floating in the river below son, his head, Lord alone knows where his head is. A stately corpse if ever I saw one, taking it nice and slow down the river like a fishing boat with all the time in the world. I didn't know what to do. I thought if I interrupt him now he's bound to be annoyed. You know me, I said nothing. Come here and let me kiss you.'

She kissed me on the forehead and pulled back to examine me. 'God, you're a fine lookin' boy. A darlin' boy. So I didn't even have a chat with him,' she went on. 'I passed up a golden opportunity for the sake of decorum. That's me all over. You know you're cute, has anyone told you you're cute yet? I'll fight to the bitter end for you son I'm tellin' you out straight, there's no love like a mother's love. So that's it, I said to myself, when I caught sight of this stately corpse, he's cut in half, so that's what the confusion is all about. God's in flitters. Have you seen my earrings?'

'No.'

'I had a lovely pair of earrings and they're gone. Your Daddy probably loaned them out. He'll loan me out next. He's given the wheelbarrow out to someone and God knows when we'll see it again, if ever.'

She stood up, one arm on the table to steady herself. Her face was strained. Why was she so tired all the time? Honestly she'd done hardly anything yet and it was half past four. You're an awful lazy bitch, she thought. Even as she thought, another part of the wall surrounding her mind caved in, the dust and slack rising like grey clouds leaving her disorientated as a spinning top. Who said that? Who said that about me? She swung around, but there was only herself in the kitchen. She clutched the side of the table for support.

It was against Ma's principles to have sex so the memory of being raped by Da was as common as combing her hair to her. It was a bad habit he couldn't get out of and she couldn't stop him, like wanting death very bad and not being able to stick a knife in your own back. (It's my secret opinion that for years he wanted her to kill him and when they weren't fencing they were wrestling over who'd kill who until they had to take a break so she could make dinner for us. They were impatient for us to hurry up and not waste time talking over the dinner because they had to get back to their wrestling match.) Ma had a will of iron when it came to getting over being raped by a caged lion. She blamed us on it because they married to have children and if it wasn't for us she'd be living in paradise right now. Once she blamed us she felt grand again. She had some nerve, that was my secret opinion but you can see why I kept it to myself. She lay still for a while tense as a cobra looking down the barrel of a shotgun. Dragging herself back to life again after the rape, she'd say, 'Damn him to hell, I'll go down and do my ironing.' Like a queen she rose majestically out of the marriage bed. She swung her legs out onto the floor and felt for her slippers under the bed like a blushing bride who'd slept with the best man on her wedding night by mistake.

Then she went across the room and looked in the mirror and said, 'Ugh.'

I saw them aching with sadness, dragging their carcasses around the house like mules in the desert looking for a watering hole. And then I saw them mad with grief because love was forbidden in our house because we were all sinners. Then Ma pretended she was a young girl and her chances were high again (ten to one) and around that time she started flirting with me. She shook the wrinkles out of her face and ran her hands down over her bony hips for me to admire. I never felt so happy in my whole life, she powdered her face and covered her cheekbones with a bright red rouge to knock thirty years off her.

'You think your mother is getting old Ben?' she asked me pinching my cheeks with two fingers like she did when I was a baby.

'Course not,' I said.

'Would you call me beautiful?' she asked.

'Beautiful,' I agreed.

'Really?'

'Really,' I said.

'And you won't leave me?'

'I won't leave.'

'Promise me.'

'I swear to God.'

Goodbye To The Woods

I was caught with my pecker in my hands just as I was about to retire. The woods had lost their appeal for me, Da said. Perhaps I was tired but the old excitement wasn't there anymore. It was an effort to undo my zip. It was an effort to pull my pecker out. My heart wasn't in it. The school children gave up coming to the woods. Perhaps they grew up. Was it the end of an era? Anyway as luck would have it on my last trip I got caught. It turned out they were after me all the time. They kept it out of the papers so I wouldn't be on the alert. It's just possible I grew careless. You should never be cocksure of anything. A schoolgirl arrived in the woods shortly after me. There was no waiting time. There was always a period of waiting. You can see how tired I was, I took no notice of this change. I see myself as an unlucky man. It's always been like that for me. I don't gamble. Why would I gamble? Had I faced up to that fact I would have known from the beginning that I was bound to get caught. The lucky ones are not put away. The lucky ones walk the streets at night and never get mugged. The lucky ones don't get buggered or beaten up. They do what they like and they walk the street free men. That's luck for you. It turned out the schoolgirl wasn't a schoolgirl after all. It turned out she was a fully grown woman. It turned out she was a screw from the slammer. It turned out the screws wanted me for questioning. They locked me up for two years. I liked it. The prison was overcrowded with socialists like myself. It was just like old times. We took what belonged to us. We marched to the beat of our own hearts. I made friends. I lost friends. I sang and danced. What more could a man ask for? I knew freedom. I tasted it. I had it for breakfast, dinner and tea. I had no worries. I had no money. Money's a curse. All too often it offends people. You have a little more than the next man and he wants to cut your throat. Here we were all equal. Some were in longer than others and that had to be taken into account. I understood that. The screws hated us. They had to worry about us all day long. They had to take sleeping pills to help them sleep. I slept like a new-born babe. They resented us. One day two of them got me in the toilets and beat me up. They wanted my new-found freedom, but I didn't give it to them. I continued to sleep well. I did twenty press-ups a day. I talked with other socialists. We shared what we had. The five year men had to get a bit extra. The ten year men a little extra than the five year men. That's why the lifers were kept in a separate pen. I understood all this. Often I handed over what I had without them having to come to me for it. I was happy, I didn't want to leave. Once out I lost my freedom. I regretted I'd ever got a taste for it. I craved it the way the next man craves drink.

The woman told me I should plan things out more. Plan for what? Every move I make is blocked by something or someone. My pecker has given up all hope. It's dead as a dodo. I see myself as an impotent man. That's what led me to other women. After the woods and my holiday in the slammer I headed back into the town. The pubs were smoky and overcrowded. I didn't like them. You had to interest yourself in other people's affairs. It was bloody murder. Strangers told me their life stories. Where they went wrong and how they were going to remedy it. How they were right and would always be right, what they would do if they were in charge of the country. On and on it went. It was hell. I knew they had no idea and yet when you're in a pub you can't say. You have to be polite. You have to act as if you believe in civilized behaviour. Fuck civilized behaviour. The one good thing about the pubs was the women. It use to be that women didn't drink in pubs, now all that is changed. They drink themselves into the sinks in the women's toilets where they throw up. What I like about women is that they don't burden you with their life story. They like to listen. They like you to make promises to them. They like you to lie to them. Some of them like you to beat them up. It makes them feel better. They like you to fool around with other women. They like quick fucks. They like you to tell them you love them. Some of them like you to tell them you're a married man. I like the younger ones. They're nice and quiet. They know their place. They don't care about their life. They think it's all ahead of them and in the meantime they'll fool around. They call it having a good time. I love women. I've always loved them. I picked one up and walked her home to her place. In between we had a quick fuck, against a wall, up a laneway. Behind the pub itself. After the fuck I took to talking. I couldn't stop talking. Sometimes they wanted me to go in with them for a coffee. I couldn't talk if they were making coffee. Then they might want to fuck again. I couldn't stop talking. It was like I was really crying. Talking seemed to be the only way I could grieve.

I see myself as a womaniser. I changed them every two weeks. I didn't want them to develop any bad habits. I didn't want them to get to know me. I just wanted to talk. After a while I fucked for their sake. It took up precious time. I started talking during it. I couldn't stop talking. I felt I was pouring bucketfulls. I couldn't understand it. They wanted to see me again. I couldn't understand that either. It lasted a few months. Then one night this woman started talking. I could see where it was leading to. One day the woman wanted to talk instead of fuck. And worse the woman wanted to talk about us. What was there to say? It might go on for years. It might never end. I stopped going to pubs. For a while strange women said hallo to me in the street. I ignored them. After a while it stopped. I was relieved. I knew I'd had a narrow escape.

When Da came out the first time he accused Ma of seeing other men. Little did he know I was the other man. Da was very vague about when Ma met other men but he felt it was whenever he wasn't there. Or else she met him at some secret rendezvous like maybe the back row in the pictures or at the end of our road there's a laneway where you could hide for hours. But according to her I was the only one good enough for her. There was something special about me she said, if there was only she could see it. Da didn't think it was the milkman or postman or anyone like that. He didn't think they'd have the balls for it. He suspected the doctor she went to once a month to collect a prescription for her nerves. He also suspected Fr. Darcy who said mass on a Sunday. He pestered her about him and finally she gave in and swore she wouldn't go to mass anymore. He calmed down for a while but unfortunately it wasn't just seeing other men that bothered him.

All the women gathered on the footpath specially in summertime for a natter. But when he came out it dawned on him that it was pretty regular whereas he'd thought she'd only talk to another woman about once a year or whenever she needed anything. He was always saying, 'Keep it down, can't ya?' The sight of two or three women gathered together and nattering nineteen to the dozen drove him wild. For a start he couldn't figure out what they were nattering about, maybe it was about him. Sometimes her hands were shaking afterwards, when she was putting the pills into her mouth. I wished I could have that sort of effect on her but it was only Da that ever made her lose her cool.

He was six months on the dole when he came home one evening red-faced with excitement and shouting at the top of his voice, 'Something's goin' to happen. I can feel it in the air.' So sure and certain was he, he was even nice to me. It went on for two whole days and died out like the way forest fires start in the summer, a complete mystery to everyone. Then he stayed in bed for most of the day, grey and sick-looking as the despair bit further into him. It was my job to sit by the side of his bed until he came out of these bouts. I didn't want to but they said. 'We gave our lives to you and you've to give your life to us, that's what family is all about.' On some things they were thick as thieves. To pass the time I read a lot because when Da wasn't in tip-top shape like a lion he bored me. I hated being too close to him as well because you could never tell with him. He opened his eyes and looked warily at me but didn't say anything. All his attention was on the wall at the foot of the bed, it was like a big screen that he could watch and imagine anything he liked on it but he didn't look as if he saw anything on it.

'Would you like a cup of tea?' I asked.

'You sound just like your Ma. Tea's the answer to everything.'

'Water?' I asked.

'You sound just like my Da use to, save the tea and burn the water,' he said, stubborn as a rock.

I got very tired and sleepy myself like a jazz song weary with the world and all who sail through it. I wasn't the sort who could say cheery things like, Cheer up, or Tomorrow will be a better day. Some of the boys call it bullshit but I think it's someone with gambling in their blood. Well, I wasn't a betting boy so I kept quiet.

'Skat,' he said. 'You drive me crazy just sitting there.'

I ran like a jack rabbit out of the room. Da often felt sorry for me like that and let me get away with things. When he was back on his feet he sat proudly in the chair fiercely determined to keep up his position as king of our house. He scratched the top of his head, splayed his legs out on the chair and planted one hand firmly on his knee. She was glad to see him back on his throne because together they could conquer the world and search for adventure on the high seas.

'You're feeling better?' she asked.

'I wouldn't say that,' he said.

'You look better,' she said.

'Have you ever seen a dead man, the way they powder up his face to take the greasy look off it? Well, he's still dead, isn't he?'

'All the same.'

Once they'd taken up fencing positions I knew they were blissfully happy.

For a while I was contented, Da said. I went for long walks in the evenings. The weather held up. My business interests grew again. As well as gardening I did a bit of house decorating. I painted walls, doors, window frames, staircases and skirting boards. You name it, I'd paint it. I had money in my pockets. I opened a post office savings account. I bought myself an extra pair of shoes. I bought a new overcoat. I even invested in a shirt and tie. I looked after the woman, a hair perm, a new skirt and cardigan. Other bits and pieces sprung up as we went along. Money made the woman happy. It was this made me realise there was nothing to her. She wasn't frightened anymore. She didn't look as faded as she use to. Our kip was clean for a change. Every morning over the breakfast table she took to smiling at me. I beat her up a few times to try and snap her out of it. She as much as told me she was happy. The woman could be bought. I didn't like it. All women could be bought. I took a turn against women. I couldn't talk anymore. I got these terrible headaches that kept me out of work for two days on the trot. I couldn't bear sunlight. I stayed in my room and told the woman to leave the food outside the door. I could hear her downstairs yapping to the boy. I warned her to be quiet. I couldn't eat. I drank a gallon of water instead. After a while I realised I was allergic to the paint. Whatever chemicals they put in it was giving me the headaches. I told the woman I'd have to drop the house decorating. I'm only healthy in a garden, I said. It was the first time I'd spoken to her in weeks. She nodded her head at me. There was a piece of dried egg on the front of the cardigan I'd bought.

I see myself as an unfortunate man. After that fiasco I got a regular job in a big house. Five days a week all through the summer, three days a week in winter. One morning I was walking up the driveway when one of the dogs came bounding down to greet me. He bit me in the leg. After all the time I'd worked there the dog failed to recognise me that particular morning. I was laid up for eight weeks. The dog was put down. They agreed to compensate me to the tune of one hundred pounds. I was a month back at work when I was laid off. These things happen. I didn't mind, as a socialist I expect injustice to be part of the daily routine of life. It confirmed my lifelong commitment. It was good for me. I was well-liked when I went on the dole. People seemed to see me in a new light. They stopped me in the street and said they'd heard what happened. They said what was happening to the world at all. They said what will become of us. In all probability everything will turn out all right, I said. I didn't believe it for one second. They patted me on the back and said drop in anytime we'd love to see you. Friends sprung up out of nowhere. People began calling to the kip for a political chat. I was popular. I was loved. I had nothing. It didn't matter. We were all alive, that's what mattered. We said so regularly. I almost laughed. I almost smiled.

After a while I noticed there were less visits then there use to be. People met me on the street and gave an excuse for not calling around. Then they dropped the excuses altogether and chatted before moving on. They were still smiling. I was still popular. I understood. Then they were in a hurry and couldn't stop. After a while they failed to recognise me. I could walk the length and breadth of the town and no one noticed I was alive. It was just as well.

PART II

Lovers Leap

Lovers Leap: And We All Leap Together

Lovers Leap: And We All Leap Together You never asked me if my name was Wallywoowoo or Fredybongbong and you never said, 'Hallo. Come 'ere, where ya come from?' From Timbuctoo if you must know, way down Bongo Land where the rivers never freeze over with ice cubes and the leaves are all crisp and tangy in your mouth. And you never asked, 'Why you stuff everything in your mouth?' Because I like eating people if you must know. And the custard and jelly and sweets and crisps and cows' meat and pigs' meat and chickens don't make up for it. They don't make up for wanting to chew on real meat and that's why I suck my finger so much but I want to suck your fingers too because all the taste is gone in mine. And I want to swallow her so bad my belly has a big ache inside from the waiting for it.

Imagine her sitting inside my belly looking out on everyone and putting her hand over her mouth to stop the spluttering giggles and I would be full up and never eat another thing until the next time I saw someone I wanted to eat. But imagine a plane crash in the middle of the desert and only two survivors and all I'll need is a knife. That's my big dream, roasting a hand, or a leg or two toes over an open fire and listening to the crackling of the meat as it cooks away merry as a thrush hopping from branch to branch. And the taste of it in my mouth as it slipped down the inside of my jaws and wet my tongue with its succulent juices before scrambling over my teeth and then the long wet trail down my throat to my waiting hungry belly. And so when Da read the murders out in the papers all I could think of was, what a bloody waste.

You can't imagine how rotten I felt because the ache inside me never went away. To read about murder is such a tease, so near yet so far.

You gave me a name but you never asked. Benee, Benjamin, it means nothing to me. You might as well have called me soap, or smoke or streetlight or bottle, because I feel nothing when I hear it. I feel nothing about soap or bottle either so where's the difference? If I become a big star I'll change my name by deed poll and call myself Lulu and the New Wave. Or the Merry Midgets if things go on the way they are. Because of course I intend to take over the band, I've no intention of hiding away in the back while plummy-arse is out front having a great time. No I'll introduce them an all and say, 'A big hand for my new band,' that will stop them getting too big for their boots.

My voice is my voice and no one is going to take it away and use it for themselves. Plummy-arse thinks that because I didn't know what to say that I'm a suck-up and he can do what he likes with me. He thought he had found his very own personal suck-up. No I have my plans all worked out and you ask anyone about a band, the voice is everything. And when I sing waistbands roll of their own accord and I have my charm as well, don't forget that. Plummy-arse will just have to put it on a stool and keep it there while I'm singing.

So I kept all my dreams to myself while Mam made a big bonfire out of hers and danced around them in a fit of rage. Did she want to get her own back or was it just an excuse to get near me? She nibbled on my ear and whispered, 'Oh Benee, Benee, lucee, lucee luscious, I love the black silk cut of your tail and your devouring ways my darling.'

It was the first inkling I had that she thought I was related to the devil. I was pretty pleased. I went upstairs immediately and sat in front of her dressing table. I waited patiently in front of the mirror to catch myself out. I had a feeling that Christ and

God and all that stuff was out the window from now on, but to look at me you wouldn't think I was that bad. I had a root through her wardrobe while I was there. I tried on a skirt and blouse and her red lipstick. Then I dabbed some of her face powder on my cheeks. I put her black high heel shoes on and took a good long look in the mirror. I was gorgeous. You can forget all I told you about my charm because if I could dress the way I wanted to I wouldn't need it. I could have popped myself into my mouth and sucked until I turned to mush. And I could see myself in Ma's clothes whereas I couldn't see myself in my own. I had her movements off to a 't' as I paraded up and down the room. I wagged my finger and gave out to myself the way she did. She loved giving out stink to me and in her clothes I could see why. I twirled around like a fashion model and fell back on the bed laughing. That was a mistake. Any sight or sound of happiness and she got angry with me.

'Ben,' I could hear her at the bottom of the stairs. 'Ben,' her high-pitched voice shrieked up at me. 'Comin',' I shouted, scrambling out of her clothes.

I put on my glum face before I went downstairs. When I opened the door she shouted, 'You're late, you're late. Get to the back of the hall quick before I throw you out altogether.' Her eyes were red and sore-looking like eyes that couldn't cry and her skin was the colour of a cold omelette, with a dull yellow matte finish. Her mouth was dry and cracked and had shrivelled up into a small round hole. She had trouble talking. She began her speech to the world and then started stuttering.

'Duhhh Duhhh Duhhhhh,' she stuttered. 'Caaa Caaa Caaa.'

'Call?' I asked her.

She shook her head and put her hand over her forehead and eyes. She curled one leg over into the other as if she was trying to lock herself together just like you do when you feel you're falling apart.

'Doa, Doaaaa, Do,dooo, Doa,' she tried again. 'Loo, loaa, looac.'

Her face was bright with shame and I felt like a rotten egg

and I jumped up suddenly, saying, 'I'll go and wash myself I'm stinkin.' I was stinking rotten all over.

'Lea, Leao, Leaaa,' she stuttered. Then she shook her head and turned her face away, putting her hand over her eyes and bending over in the chair as if she was going to be sick. I tore upstairs because by this time I was stinking from head to foot. I pulled the clothes off me, ran water into the basin and scrubbed at myself with the small nail brush to try and get the dirt off me. I tried thinking up things to say to her, Cheer up; Smile, go on smile, sunshine; Dress up in something nice. But that would only make her happy and we didn't like to be reminded of that. We were very suspicious of happiness. If it affected us it would change us overnight into people we'd never seen before. And then you would want more and more of it and people might start asking you questions about yourself and find out something about you. I winced at the thought of being that close to anyone. When I went back downstairs Ma was curled up in the chair and I went over and whispered softly in her ear, 'I love you. I love you.' A peaceful smile spread across her tired face. It was tough keeping in everyone's good books. I sat down on the floor beside her and lay my head on her lap for a while.

Ma's Holiday

It was Monday morning. The bath water was on for a hot bath. My clothes were laid out neatly on the back of the chair. My coat was downstairs on the hook on the back of the door. My high-heeled shoes were out on the landing. My scarf was neatly folded in the drawer of the dressing table by the window. This is my day, I thought, no matter what else happens this is my day. *'Don't dilly dally on your way to hell'* I'd sing as I lay waiting for the alarm to go off. I crawled down to the bottom of the bed, out over his feet and onto the floor. I shook myself as I would the sweeping brush. *'I know where I'm going and I know who's comin' with me,'* I sang aloud as I marched barefoot to the bathroom. He didn't stir, or blink an eye to acknowledge the gauntlet I flung down at him first thing every morning. GET UP. GET UP. SHAKE A LEG. I filled the bath and eased myself down into it. I lay in it a while and then I washed quickly without taking any pleasure in it. I dried myself off and cleaned the bath out with a soft cloth before returning to the bedroom.

'Joe. Joe. Get up,' I commanded him. 'It's after nine.'

He stirred, turned on his side facing the wall and ignored me. In the last few weeks he had taken to getting up later and later.

'Joe why don't you get up and go down for a paper?'

I tried again. 'It's a lovely day out,' I said. He didn't stir. Oh God what was I to do with him? What was I to do if he didn't get up at all?

I walked down the hall, down the stairs and into the kitchen. I went back upstairs and got the photo album out of the drawer and came back down again. I pored over the old photographs, filling up the hunger inside me with memories of old times. I turned swift as a hawk with the bed of a thousand thistles inside me, he was upstairs in bed. It was twelve o'clock and he was still on my patch. Every sound he made, or didn't make, made me feel sick and I was unable to eat. I needed a space to live in and he was taking it away from me. I folded my arms about myself trembling with the need for something. Oh if only he could come and put his arms around me, sneak up behind me and whisper, Love, love, my darling love in my ear. Love, love, where is love? I laid my forehead against the window pane to cool the feverish pain that sprang from the lack of it. Being deprived of love made me nervy and tense and I dragged hard on the cigarette, sucking the smoke in as if trying to blot out the gnawing absence of it. I heard him moving about upstairs, the movement like a rumble through my deadened senses, disturbing my tight grip on the room where nothing could fly or walk without my say so, but he'll have to go, thinking of him as a cockroach, an ant, my senses disturbed with him.

My floor. Look after your property and it can't be taken away from you, I scrubbed with this definite, certain purpose in mind. I'm taking care of my floor aren't I. There's never a speck of dirt on my floor. I jumped up, ran over to the drawer, took the small sharp knife out for peeling the vegetables and pocketed it. There now. Back down on my knees, scrubbing my floor, I tell you, my floor, if he comes through that door with not an ounce of respect, acting as if he owns the place, HE OWNS THE PLACE, I'll knife him in the belly. I can look after myself, oh yes I can. I got up, felt the outside of my apron pocket, the sharp wedged shape of the knife. To defend myself no matter what, to care so much about myself that I was prepared to kill another for my survival. I scrubbed on, I mean was life worth that? Was I worth that much? No I wasn't, I wasn't worth that much. I got up, went over to the press, put the knife back in the drawer. Through an opening in my mind a voice got in and said to me, 'You deserve everything you get, you bad bad bitch.' I whirled back against the press. It was him wasn't it? It was him that spoke to me. Cautiously I went out into the hall. Keeping my back to the wall, moving inch by inch down towards the staircase, I made one leap from the hall wall to the inside wall of the staircase and slowly, cautiously made my way upstairs. On the last step I stood transfixed. There was no sound from inside the bedroom. Is he dead? I thought. I turned my attention to the landing window. You could see in through that window. I inched my way along the wall hardly daring to breathe. I peered out. No one was looking in. The window's clear, but they could put a ladder up against the wall and be up in a jiffy. I listened. I heard the creaking of bedsprings. I couldn't bear waiting any longer. I opened the door like a thief and tiptoed past the bed. I opened the drawer, got my scarf out of it and closed the drawer without a squeak. Back around, shush, tiptoe past, shush, I just want my scarf. I made it to the door, closed it quietly behind me. I waited for the shame to pass, shook myself briskly, turned and hurried down the stairs again.

When I was ready the fluttering excitement of dove coos rose and flapped against the inner walls of my belly again. As I was going out the front door I called up to him, 'Get up for Christ's sake, it's dinner time.'

The excitement grew on me as I walked into town. And it wasn't any old scruff place I was going to. The doctor was not the muck. He was an educated person, a sophisticated man of the world. He was successful in his life, why you could tell by looking at him, he was. Always the neatest and smartest of suits, his hair properly cut. I walked with an increasing urgency in my step. To be one of the middle classes was a dream that hadn't come true for me, so to rub shoulders instead would have to do.

Every month of the last year he had said the same thing when I went to see him. He asked me how I was but the sudden interest in my welfare had an unsettling effect on me. Oh no first he pointed to the chair, 'Take a seat Mrs Crawford. I'll be with you in a minute.' Yes, that's how he started off each time.

I'm in the presence of a real gentleman, a well-known authority on health and probably many other matters as well, I thought. Every time I told him it was my nerves, and every time he said 'This is the last prescription Mrs Crawford. You can't keep taking these.'

Taking them like they were smarties, I thought lovingly. Oh yes I can doctor. Them pills is the best thing that ever happened to me in my life. They soothe me down and make me feel rested. And they don't ask me for things I can't give, haven't got to give. I was right fond of the doctor's room. He tried to probe into my life again the last time I went to him but I shut up like a clam.

'I'm not myself.'

'I feel tense.'

'It's my age doctor.'

That's all the information I would give. Rubbing shoulders with the comfortable helped me forget for a little while but a man was a man no matter where he came from.

I felt quite cheered up as I turned into the doctor's surgery. I walked into the waiting room and sat down beside another woman. Out of the corner of my eye I watched her, wondering whether she was approachable to talk and what kind of talk? The sweet bird of hope nestled up cosily inside me. 'I'll feed you soon my darling, I'll feed you soon.'

'Lovely day out Missis,' I said. 'You waitin' to see the doctor?'

I sneaked into the jungle to find gold and diamonds to bring back to her. I might even build a new house on another road and carry her off into the sunset like a knight in shining armour. I walked down the road to the nearby shop and flung the door open and said, 'This is a hold up. Stick 'em up.'

'What'll it be?' the woman said.

'A bottle of orange,' I said.

'You want a straw with it?'

'Yes please.'

She had a bottle opener under the counter and when she opened it she slid it dangerously across the drab dingy counter as if to say, 'Have a drink partner, it's thirsty weather.'

When I came outside I saw David Byrne and Charley Brittan leaning against the wall of the shop. I thought they were going to jeer me and call me Mammy's boy like they usually did but they were too busy thinking so I stretched my legs out in a bowlegged stance, my hips swaying with the heavy butt of the revolvers against them. I adjusted the heavy leather belt across my waist and screwed my eyes up into the sunset, took a drag on the cigarette hanging from my wet surly lips before spitting on the ground.

'Cincinnatti Kid,' Dave called over.

'Nope.'

''Twas so. Saw it on Sunday.'

I waited until I'd passed them before shouting over my shoulder, 'Sunday before, Jack Asses.'

I was relieved I had got by without being jeered but I didn't push my luck by hanging around. My brother Andy was the first one to call me a Mammy's boy. We were in the school yard one day playing marbles and even though I was four years younger I was winning a mountain of marbles off him. But Andy got ugly about me winning and started pushing me around the yard saying, 'Ah sure you're only a Mammy's boy anyways.' It spread like wildfire around the school yard and ever after that's what they all called me.

I hung around the road to see if any other boy I knew came along but they were all off fighting wars and saving lives and pulling people out from under heaps of rubble after a big earthquake somewhere. Besides I was busy looking for gold and diamonds. I hung around a while longer because you never know what might happen. The sun was hot enough to make me cranky tired. It scorched the top of my head, it almost burnt right through and left me with a big round hole but I stuck it out so I'd know what it was like to be tortured. I could feel the blisters coming out on my lower lip, my face was going to be raw meat the next morning but I would be all the stronger for it. Around teatime I gave up torturing myself and headed on home. I charged our front gate on my white stallion and spliced through the wooden bars with my sword to get inside. I charged up the front path, dismounted and used the dustbin as a post to tie the horse up. I went around the side of the house and squatted down against the wall for a quick smoke. They weren't too happy about my smoking. They said it would stop me growing but that was a lie because I'd stopped growing around ten years of age anyway. It was ten to one I was going to be a dwarf.

Ma pestered me to tell her I loved her because if she asked him he'd beat her. Da had contempt for anyone on two legs on account of everybody was born with original sin on their souls. He thought that the church was behind him and were egging him on to beat her into improving herself because she was such a sinner. All this sort of stuff seemed to come to me when I was smoking as if I was secretly meditating on the mystery of life whenever they weren't around. Before I stubbed my cigarette out I pictured her stark naked, then I plunged indoors in the nick of time as a stray bullet whizzed past and nicked my ear.

'No luck today,' I said to her.

'No luck?' she asked.

'Yeah, no luck.'

'Ah never mind pet,' she said.

'It's too hot out,' I said. 'Maybe tomorrow.'

'Where's all your friends today.'

'Friends huh! What friends,' I said mockingly. 'I've got no friends.'

'Now, now that's not like you. You just missed them did you?'

'Yeah I suppose.'

'You're too young for cynicism pet. Your whole life's ahead of you.'

'What life?' I said, imitating Da. I put a look on my face as if I was going to blow my brains out any minute.

'Now Ben. Things aren't that bad.'

'So what,' I said.

'Don't be cheeky you.'

Just to get her back I thought of the two of them doing it and making the usual mess not like in the pictures where they have a candlelit dinner first and he proposes a little nightcap on the moonlit terrace before the event. I was disappointed I hadn't come up with the goods and I was angry I'd built her hopes up only to dash them to the ground like that.

Before Da went on the dole he warned me there would be no work for me when I left school. 'Things have changed, they're not what they were before,' he said, brilliant analytical stuff like that but I'd already decided to be an artist so it was no skin off my nose. 'It doesn't matter,' I said. 'I'm goin' to be an artist.'

Da's eyes rolled wildly around in his sockets at that. He looked over at her for inspiration because she was in charge of all the good ideas in our house. She shrugged her shoulders as if she'd never heard of an artist before.

'A cabaret star or a film star,' I said enlightening her. 'Or maybe a painter. Or a director of pictures. A banjo player maybe.'

He slumped forward in the chair and moaned as if I'd struck a sword through his back like a clever coward. 'Oh Jesus Christ, Oh Jesus Christ he's an egghead,' he kept repeating.

'Gardener,' he hissed. 'An electrician. A brickie. Factory worker. What's wrong with factory work?' he hissed.

'It's just not for me,' I said. This crippled him altogether. He couldn't breathe and he couldn't walk on account of me. Ma had to help him upstairs so he could lie down. I always had a tremendous effect on people, even in school the teacher use to pick on me for special punishments. It was this special effect I had that gave me the bright idea of being an artist. If I could do it to one maybe I could do it to a thousand. The odds were that I'd end up being promiscuous and make Ma jealous into the bargain.

I spun my hands above my head shaping stars and twirling moons, love is Mammy's kiss and Daddy's moans, son you'll still love us won't ya? Ya won't forget us will ya? You're all we have, promise you won't forget us?

'I'm afraid I will,' I taunted them.

'Oh son, oh son, I was beside myself,' Ma said. Overnight I changed from a girl into a woman. I noticed it first in my hands. I had strong thick lumps of hands that could squeeze the life out of another man's throat before breakfast. They grew thinner and spiky-looking and all my fingers were covered in nicotine. I'm not a heavy smoker and if I was I'd use the side of a match box to rub the stuff off. They were definitely the helpless hands of a woman. If you can't kill, stay still, that was my first thought upon waking. Then I got out of bed and had a look in the mirror. I was a middle-aged housewife. My looks were gone, my body had collapsed into a mould of shapeless flesh. I say my looks were gone but I couldn't actually remember ever having any. It's possible other people noticed them and remarked to me. You can't take note of everything yourself. Lucky is the woman who can recall her life in all its finer details. I'm hard put to remember I'm still alive. I hid myself in a skirt and jumper that was far too big for me. I had a terrible need of a cigarette. I found a half used box of cigarettes in my apron pocket. 'God be praised,' I murmured as I lit up. My hands trembled so much that I had to light the match, hold my hand with my other hand and guide it up to the cigarette that was dangling from the ends of my lower lip. That was another thing, my mouth had shrunk overnight into a pinched little ball of rage. My lips were so dry I could feel the flakes sticking to the tip of the cigarette. That reminded me that I was pulling on the butt and in danger of burning my lips. I lit up again. Before I put the kettle on the gas for a cup of tea I realised that I'd turned into a chain smoker.

The facts of life have nothing to do with sex. No one is interested in sex but we're all forced to do it.

Tell your children nothing about it son, God knows they're not missing anything. There is only one fact of life that matters; you are stuck with yourself. Did I tell my children that? I'm so forgetful it's possible it slipped my mind. Anyway by now they've found out and if they haven't they should be ashamed of themselves. I was filled with a sudden feeling of dread and I hid in a corner of the kitchen. The world was about to blow up into smithereens with one of their new bombs and I'd be left without a cigarette to my name. Then I realised that was too easy, whatever was about to happen would be slow and tortuous and I'd live to see it all through. You can imagine the state I'd be in but who cares about that I'd be breathing, no gasping and begging for the death that had no intention of coming. In short, I would suffer again. As I huddled in a corner of the kitchen I heard a voice coming from upstairs.

'Is my breakfast ready yet?' It was him making an enquiry about the state of play in the kitchen. I sprung from the corner as if catapulted by an unseen hand towards the cooker.

'God be praised,' I murmured as I cracked the egg into the frying pan slid two rashers down beside it. He sat opposite me and somewhere about we listened to the murmuring of our sons. He's a handsome man and I'm eternally grateful he lowered himself to marry me. He could have had anyone. Women fall at his feet as he goes by them. I love him. I've always loved him. He loves me. His looks are still there after all this time. As I remember I was a very plain faced girl with sallow skin and thin wispy hair. My mother was worried no one would marry me. Life is tough when you're plain. A brain is no substitute for a pretty face and as it happened I had neither. I couldn't understand why a handsome man like my husband even looked my way. It forced me to believe in miracles. God in his infinite mercy felt sorry for me.

My husband should have gone into politics. With a face like his everyone would vote for him. The only problem is that he's a socialist. He's a stubborn man too, once he makes his mind up about something nothing will change it. If he could keep his mouth shut he would do well. He thinks everyone wants to be equal to everyone else. I couldn't tell him what a bloody fool he was. He wouldn't like it, I wouldn't like having to tell him. Why should I tell him? The poor man is full of illusions of one sort or another. He doesn't understand that the winners of this world are the extremists. It doesn't matter what you say when you are an extremist just as long as it's next to impossible because the world loves a good challenge. My husband is a Christian whereas I'm an atheist. He was always tortured by the thought of God. Is he or isn't he? Will he or won't he? He broke his heart worrying about God whereas I take a delight in praying and I'm a regular churchgoer as well. I love the church, it's the one place I can rest up. No one can disturb you there. You don't have to put on a show or try to fight your corner the way you do when you're talking to someone. God doesn't care what you look like, he doesn't care what you say. He doesn't care what you do. He does not ask questions. It's plain as the nose on my face he isn't there. I love praying to him. I love to sing his praises. God gave me a sense of humour. I love him for what he is. My husband still wrestles with the problem of God from time to time. Yes, he turned him into a problem whereas I turned him into a friend.

I don't like talking to people. The effort to keep up with what people are saying is too much for me. For a start they expect me to believe them. I believe no one. My mother told me stories about my father that would make your hair stand on end. She expected me to believe every word she said. In the end she said not only was I plain as ditchwater but she didn't like the look on my face either. Disbelief made me unpopular all round. I taught myself to hide it. I even forgot about it. My handsome husband has never seen a look of disbelief on my face. He thinks I'm interested in what he has to say. Some days he talks non-stop. I pray to God he will find work soon because he drives me crazy with his talk. He thinks I adore him. He thinks I love him. The truth is I am indifferent to him. I wish he would drop dead and leave me alone. I could love him if he was dead.

He wants us to travel to a socialist country so he can see what it's like at close range. Some days it's on the tip of my tongue to tell him that people would die rather than be equal to each other but I say nothing. I like my privacy. I like to be quiet. He hates me because he doesn't understand me. He is a mouth, why am I not a mouth? That's what he thinks equality is. Is it any wonder my nerves are gone. After he'd left the house I sat alone in the kitchen. Some day I may have a sneaking regard for myself. I may even come to like myself. I've tried to train myself into liking myself. I've tried to force myself. I even tried to fool myself. It was no use. The truth will not lie down. And worse yet, the truth will not die. Some days are worse than others, I'm grateful for small mercies. Once I ran out into the middle of the road with a large truck heading straight for me. The truck driver swerved to avoid me. He ended up in hospital while I lay completely untouched in the middle of the road. The world is full of gentlemen. They are all wonderful. Nothing will do them but that they hold a door open for you or give up their seat on a bus. They think I can do nothing for myself. They think I am helpless. I say nothing. They took me into hospital and treated me for shock anyway. Anything you want to know about hospitals just send a stamped addressed envelope and I'll reply by return of post. I strongly recommend them. It's the one place in the world you can be sure of being looked after. Breakfast, dinner and tea is served on a tray, could you ask for any more than that? A priest came to see me every other day. He said much the same things I had said to myself. Life was wonderful. Life was a precious gift. My whole life was ahead of me. It was against every law in the book to try and kill myself, he said. He asked me for a good reason. When he came down off his high horse, he said, 'Well give me some sort of a reason.'

The least I could do was answer him. 'I've no reason,' I said.

I could see by the look on the poor man's face that his love for humanity was disappearing up the spout.

'But why then?' he asked me.

I thought of playing around with him, my mother didn't love me enough, my father was an alcoholic, there were pigs in the parlour and so on but I was too tired for games. I felt lower than I'd ever felt before. Once again I'd failed to achieve what I'd set out to do.

I shrugged my shoulders. 'It's always been like that,' I said.

I was surprised he was so keen to see me go on living. He came again the next day. He took a great interest in family life, it was probably because he was a bachelor. I told him about my sons. My sons are vulgar and healthy and they love to curse. All men take up cursing at one time or other. I have no preferences, if I feel like cursing I indulge myself and then forget about it. I tried to love my sons but it was too much for me. I've no trouble with strangers though. Strangers are wonderful, I love strangers.

I love the nurses in the hospital. I will never forget them in my prayers. They never complained when I refused to eat. They didn't deny me my rights. My mother denied me my rights. She forced me to eat. The nurses respected my rights. They pleaded with me and then they sent for *him*. He threatened to kill me himself if I didn't eat. He took the good out of it, I'll never forgive him for that. But I always try to look on the bright side of things, so far I've managed to avoid suffering too much. I'm against suffering of any kind, I think it should be banned or else concentrated in one area so the rest of us can live in peace. The doctor was a handsome man. My husband was nothing compared to him. He gave me tablets to calm me down. The tablets did the trick. On the whole I felt nothing all day long. It was wonderful. I was a happy woman at long last. Within a short space of time I found I couldn't live without my tablets. It's the same with humans. You become fond of someone and then find you can't do without their company. I never managed to give up the tablets or the cigarettes. My only success was with humans. I have learned to ignore them. I fall asleep in the middle of a chat. You can rely on most people to take a hint. They know when they're not wanted. Scram. The tablets made me lose my appetite. Then I came up with a good idea, I'd go on strike as opposed to just giving up eating to die. You read about strikes in the papers every night of the week. Every man in the country has been on strike at one time or another, it was about time a woman had a go at it. I gave up eating again but this time with a definite purpose in mind. I can't tell you how excited I was at the prospect of starving myself to the bitter end. At last I'd kill myself and with any luck make a wonderful husband sit up and take notice of me.

My sons didn't seem to notice anything different about me. I was always thin but within weeks I'd withered away to a stick. It was only when I took to the bed that they started complaining. As it turned out my wonderful husband was away at the time, living it up in a hotel. He tried to force me to believe it was the slammer. I never believed him. I knew he was only trying to get me down. I was too busy starving myself to death to check him out. Eventually one of the boys went to a neighbour. She phoned for a doctor. I ended up in my beloved hospital bed again. This time he refused to leave the hotel to come and see me. It was too plush where he was, he said.

The doctor said I was a very unusual woman. It was young girls that usually went on strike, they said. I didn't give in to the flattery. I'll never give in to anything. Middle aged women are broken by the time they lose their looks. They retire to the kitchen. Not me. I'd like to live beside the graveyard, then they can throw me over the wall when the time comes. I don't want to be a bother to anyone. I don't want to cause unnecessary expense. It was the longest strike in the history of womankind. I was making up for lost time. I'm ashamed to say my beloved doctors bullied me back to life again. I was going great guns when they turned nasty. They put a plate of food down in front of me and one of them sat by my side until I gave in. The truth was they didn't come into it. I was as tired dying as living. The effort was too much for me. I was helpless one way or another.

It's a long time since I cried. To my knowledge I've yet to know the pleasure of it. He says I've a heart of stone. I'm proud of that. I'd like to frame that remark and put it over the fireplace. 'Here sits a woman with a heart of stone.' What wonderful news. One night over the dinner table he announced to my sons and myself that I was cold as ice. He was loving it. 'She's hard as nails,' he went on.

That's him all over, he shovels it on with a trowel and then everyone loses interest. I told him to be subtle, to choose one remark and slip it in every so often and cry as he said it so they'd see the effect it was having on him. But he ignored my advice. The result was my sons wouldn't believe him. They began finding fault with him. They compared me to a saint and him to a dog. All sons have a soft spot for their mothers, it's just as well. They sang my praises in front of him. To get back in favour with them he began boasting about our sex life. He paced the floor as he spoke.

'We begin with a series of mutters,' he said.

What were the mutters? My sons demanded to know.

'Nice evenin', was one,' he said. *'What time is it?'* was another.

'More,' they said, 'tell us more.'

'Did you put the bin out? was another,' he said.

But my sons were disappointed, they expected the heavens to burst open.

'And then I fuck her,' he said cheerfully, that's the bit he liked you see. 'And sometimes I give her a few clatters to add spice to the grand affair.'

My sons turned to me for guidance. Where did I come into it? I squirmed in the chair. 'I lie there and take it,' I told them.

'But what do you do?' they chorused. 'You must do something.'

'I pull his trousers down,' I said after a while. 'His toes get caught in the turn-ups. Or his knee won't give way to the cloth. I help him to come,' I said. That went down well. Their mother sacrificed herself. Their mother was a saint after all. By now they should have guessed the truth for themselves.

My head cleared. I came back to myself. I knew things I'd never known before but I couldn't remember what they were. It was something to do with the woman before she forced me to marry him. Things she'd never told me and yet I knew about them. I was mystified at that. After a while I put it out of my mind, there were more important things to be thinking about than her. Whew! That was a close one.

She came into my room to tuck me in, rolling me over like a carcass of meat out of the butcher's shop. Fluffing up the bedclothes, fluffing me down under them.

'My little wizard,' she bent over and kissed me before pushing me in against the wall to flatten out the creases on the sheets and make it fresh looking. 'You is me, I is you,' in a wave of passion she half lifted me back into the centre of the bed.

'You slide me around like a bar of bloody soap,' I complained. I lay proud and uncomfortable in the bed. A uniform of splendour covered me, one with gold plaited braids running from the shoulder to the cuffs. It was dark blue with silver buttons and my hat was the same colour, tall and shaped like the bottom of an upturned boat with braiding along the top edge. It was me in *Mutiny on the Bounty*.

'Leave me alone,' I said. But she wouldn't. I was hers and if another woman ever came within an ass's distance of me she'd knife her.

'You're still only a child,' she reminded me solemnly. And then in a commanding voice, 'Remember that you twirp.' She patted my hair, flicking my silken fringe off my forehead.

'Poor, poor Ben,' she said softly. 'How are ya feeling love?'

I turned my head away from her so she wouldn't see into my eyes. . . . Courtly smiles at little boys down the road, a subdued mouth that never pouts except in private, a tone of voice – come here, my boys – low and keening, seldom heard above the shouts of others, weaving trails of names along the bitter iron gates and hands that preach This life's a peach if you're born a leech on a cloud of silver lining. Flashing eyes that seek out lice in heads of boys that never heard of courtly smiles or loving hands to iron out lines on faces, faces painted light as white standing in the doorways of the barns. A swinging gait that aped the ladle she had scooped to spoon the soup, an image of a hand that spanned my waist, kissed my neck and whispered in my ears, 'Son, she always called to me, in tears.' Weeping for the massacre of life, wailing down the laneway of the years – no one hears, no one hears. The heart without a spear to gouge it out and jab it blindly at the air – take that you louts. . . .

'I feel awful,' I said prematurely.

She looked down at me with a cruel hard face as she patted my hair down over my egg-shaped skull. Her face pale, but long and wider-looking, the hub of light from the window making her look like a strong alert woman. And she crooned me a lullaby to help me sleep. As she stood up to go, she bent over again to ruffle my hair in a tide of kindly waves. 'You couldn't feel awful at your age pet. It's not possible.'

Filled with the flow of kindness, the sweetness of her nature opening out like a flower to the sun for an instant I could see the mystery of my Ma, the indivisibility of her soul, the gracefulness of her sidelong glance as she met my eyes across the space where the lies turned to flies and circled around her face or flattened to the ground with her heel – 'There another, lie down.' Between the table and the sink she spun them out like the piper with his flute, that elusive quality of light that dances through the night and never sheds a single light in spite of all the promises and might, that strength that never slackened and never lost sight of the sheer delight in the grandeur of the lies. The pressure on her lips to meet the world head-on with the most astounding whoppers, to lead the watchers on down dead-end lanes and bypass the scarecrows in the fields, those infidels with bright and cheery waves, reassuring the company around her – and here we have the leaders of the maze. They know how to judge the hunger and its hate, the thirst that never slakes its vengeance from the soldiers iron-cast alibi of freedom and the state. My Ma yawned over evening papers, licking her lips at treacherous lies from across the ruins of fate – Yes I do agree. Oh most certainly I do agree. And was it just a trick of light that made me think my Ma winked as if she knew what made me tick or was the wink another lie? I turned over on my back and glared the ceiling up to meet the sky, sullenly replied though she wasn't there, 'I'm just a slave to you, Ma. A rotten filthy slave.' And now the truth was out, for sneaking from my belly to my back all summer long the same remark – What am I to do with myself? followed by the pleading tones that made me feel I was a mouse and she a hare running from the hound. 'Tell me what to do. For God's sake tell me what to do, Ma.'

I took another cigarette out of my trouser pocket and lit up. It was as if she could see up through the ceiling for she was out in the hall just as I started to puff, puff.

'Ben. Ben. I hope you're not smoking up there.'

'Course not,' I called down. 'I'm reading a comic.'

'Your Da said he saw you out smoking yesterday. It's that cough you have, your Da says it's definitely a smoker's cough.'

'It's a ordinary cough.'

'No pet. I said that to your Da, its a cold cough, a summer cold I said. Everyone gets them these days, but he said no it's a smoker's cough.'

'Don't mind him Ma. It's a little cough I picked up from another fellow, that's all.'

'I don't know pet. He says it's disgraceful to have a smoker's cough at your age.'

'Honest to God, Ma, if I was smokin' I'd tell you.'

'You would, wouldn't you son. You wouldn't keep anything back from me. You tell me everything don't you?'

'Course I do. I always tell you everything.'

She gave a big black sigh up the stairs after me. 'I don't know what to think. Your Da says one thing, you another.' She gave a big black sigh again. 'You would tell me wouldn't you?'

'What?'

'If you were smoking, you'd tell me wouldn't you?'

'Course I would.'

When she passed messages on from Da like that I lost all patience with her. I was sure the message was all wrong from the start. He wouldn't notice if I came home drunk, never mind have a smoke. She had boiled the message down in her mind until it was no more than a stringy bit of meat. But Da was trying to tell me something, I was sure of that. Was he trying to warn me of some danger? Was he in some way trying to solve my problems and if he was, what was it? I puffed hard on the cigarette. She doted on me far more than she had my two brothers. I was her dote and the other two had always fumed with jealousy over it. I didn't feel they were my brothers any more on account of her. It wasn't easy being a dote and I hadn't asked for it either. She brought me up as an example to my brothers which only made them hate me all the more. I didn't ask to be an example to others, I bore all her fussing over me regally but this summer my patience was coming to an end. But what did Da really say? Did he send his regards through her voice? Did he send his love through her hands? And did he send his advice down through her mind to my mind? Did he want to talk to me? Did he want to kiss me? Did he want to hold me close in his arms. What did Da say?

'Fuck,' he said. 'Fuck, fuck, fuck.'

That's what Da said. The word fuck, rose to his throat like wild fowl flying through the air and when it rolled onto his lips he heard the shotguns exploding in his ears and the thump and thud of the dead fowl on the driven earth. He witnessed the men driven like cattle, used for fodder for the money over and over again until they fell by the wayside, left to drown in the pool of their own blood for a dead man was worth nothing. And he with them, a sucker for an easy buck, no skills, no trade, tut tut, you're born in the wrong shop Daddyo. His eyes rolled and pitched in his sockets, the back of his neck moist and clammy with the fat fingers of terror pinching into him as he stood in the dole queue with the other men. He sunk to the footpath in the town with the weight of despair. He slunk into a shop doorway and a minute came and went and snuggled into his ears without speaking and cradled him where he was a mystery and small and squeaking like a silver bead, a minute was his real woman and she fondled without speaking to him and slapped his back to iron his muscles out and take away the rusty pains that made him so vicious. 'Minute' made him smile and her foxgloves powdered him all over so his skin smelt fresh and scented as garden flowers and his hands fluttered like butterflies.

Ma took two of her smarties and sat by the window listening to the voices floating in off the roadway. She checked her nails over. She took the emery board from her apron pocket and filed them down. All my beauty is gone to my nails, she thought. She slipped the emery board in front of the cigarettes in her pocket. 'No one ever touched me in my life,' she said aloud, rising and rhythmical, full and timorous with the memories creaking around in her mind again. Her dark brown eyes flashed and a pink blush came to her cheeks like a hand tenderly pinching her. Stillness and love with faint sounds in the distance, she would not be rushed, fussed or bothered by anything ever again. She looked lovingly at herself in the mirror. Such a feast of peace and love coming in all directions, every pore opened to receive the oil like fluid that made her feel alive. She would always be there for us, she would never go away in case we needed her. A mother never moves or changes her mind, she took another smartie just in case. Her body was so slight her footprints were like the brush of a feather on the earth. A dim image of human-ness with a thin strip of flesh on her bones. The stoop of her back was as if a giant hand was moulding her, shaping her in readiness for the earth's mouth.

My Gran's hair turned white as the tablecloth at the last supper.

'Where's Jack, girlie?' she asked Ma. 'He put his arms around me and said, Verone, Oh Verone.' He called me Verone, I ask you. I love you, he said, but I shook him away like I would a clap of thunder. You turned my hair white, I said, you broke the skin of my lip. You locked me in the back room in a fit of jealousy. Love I said, don't be codding yourself. You don't know what love is Jack. When he went away to war I pressed his uniform for him and sewed the gold buttons on the front of his jacket. I put my cracked lip up against his ear, my voice was silky and soothing and I kept saying to him, Leave no stone upturned out there Jack. It's good exercise for you. It keeps you fit and well and brings the colour back to your cheeks. 'Where's Jack?' she asked Ma. 'I want my Jack.'

'He's vanished into thin air,' Ma replied.

When Da got back from town he stood by the gate on the off-chance of a chat with a passing cronie. He couldn't chat with her because she was not to be trusted. His need to chat was pressing in on him, becoming sharp as a toothache and he feared he'd hightail it and go whingeing to her. He held onto the wall with both hands in case his legs took out from under him and around the back of the house to her. 'Whoa there,' he spoke soft to himself. 'Stay in there till it passes.' Pass in under the bridge of dreams and become a hazy thought of a desire one time to talk to a tart. To talk low and serious under the sixty-watt bulb, her one side of the kitchen table, he the other. It would turn into a bloody interrogation, it always did. Where were you? Who were you out with this time? He whelped in pain and leaned over the wall. Not a cronie in sight, up nor down the bloody road. The need to immerse himself in a bath of talk, thick as thieves talk, soft as butter on the tongue, it was so powerful that every tooth in his mouth pained him. How can you talk to a cream puff, a doughnut with arsenic sprinkled on top?

'Whoa there,' he spoke soft to himself. 'Stay on in there, it'll pass.' He held on the natural rhythms of it now bunched up inside him like the knots of bark on a tree. Slowly the rhythms dissolved and he sighed with relief. He turned triumphantly and went down by the side of the house. She could go fuck herself.

When he came in she adjusted the collar of her apron and fiddled with the ends of it. She gave him a shy nervous glance and was filled with the wonder of him for he looked so sure and firm in himself while she stood on the earth shaking like a jelly-baby.

The Raging Of The Queen

Listen to me, she said. I took my first drink on the eighth of June 1980. It was a scorcher of a day and it was working up to a fine summer. I could hear the bees humming through the open window and the peaceful atmosphere that comes with heat seemed to calm me down. I remember the date and the day well, not for the drink but for the mood I was in. It was as if I had come to the end of something and there was no going back for me. What happened was I was sitting in the chair looking out at the day when all of a sudden I stood up and shouted out, 'I'm pissed-off.' Well it's not like me to talk back, never mind shout. As luck would have it, he wasn't there. I went upstairs and sat down in front of the dressing table. A ravishing beauty stared back at me, I was at least safe with that much on my side. I got the powder puff and pressed some powder onto my nose in case it came out in a sheen. Then I changed out of my skirt into my good dress and cardigan and last of all, my ruby red lipstick for my juicy lips. Everyone I knew drank too much when I was a child. When I think of the grown-ups then, I think of them all staggering westwards, or southbound and some of them heading east, staggering like babies only learning to walk. As a result I never touched a drop until the day I got pissed-off.

I felt brazen as you like in the middle of the afternoon heading straight for a pub. But I was right to go there for it was cool and quiet at that hour of the day. It's not in my nature to step out of line but the day I did I felt six feet tall. Of course I felt awkward, a woman on her own like that, but I thought to myself as I sipped my first glass of stout, it's better to break out than to die wondering. Being alone made me feel very small and empty inside as if I wasn't really there. I suppose I wasn't use to it. I'm sure if you stay on your own long enough you begin to feel a bit bigger in yourself. I felt dreamy and distant after the glass of stout and you could say anything to me and I would laugh at you. In the beginning I went once a week. It made the rest of the week bearable and I was more cheerful in myself and the 'shush now' and the 'Ah sure it doesn't matter' out of me would make a cat sing. After about six months I met Sheila Gifney in the pub. Sheila was all over me from the word go. If you said anything to her she'd say, 'Sure aren't you great' and she'd lean over in the pub in broad daylight and give me a kiss on the cheek for myself, and when I'd say, 'For God's sake Sheila hold onto yourself' she'd look around the pub lift her glass up 'Three cheers, let them all fuck themselves, fiddlers an all' she'd say and the two of us would sit there like schoolgirls giggling and talking about nothing at all and loving every minute of it.

It was the only time I ever really relaxed and I cherished those afternoons as things began to get worse for us. Sheila told me stories that would make your hair stand on end. She remarked one day that I was like a little bird, and 'you know,' she said, 'it's great to have someone take an interest in you and listen. Really listen,' she said, leaning over until we were forehead to forehead. 'Most people don't listen to a bloody word you're saying but you're different. You're special,' she said and then she gave me the gentlest kiss, so gentle that it made me cry because no one had ever cared about me like that in my whole life. And you would never think her capable of it either for she was a big rough-looking woman and the curses out of her were fierce. I swear she was as powerful as any man ever was.

When he went away I took to going twice a week. I had one day with Sheila and one day with myself. Everything seemed to defeat me and be too much for me at that time. Even before I got up in the morning I was exhausted. Life is like that, isn't it? It wears you out when you're not looking. It was around the time there was a piece in the paper about him, it said he was messing young children around up in the woods. None of the women would talk to me on the street after it. When they saw me coming they would cross over to the other side or look right through me as if I was a pane of glass. It made me feel very shaky and twice as lonely in myself. It's funny how people can make you feel you're not alive, aren't you bad enough at it yourself? I couldn't make head nor tail of what it said in the papers about him. More likely then not they got the wrong man. There's no justice in this world, there never was and there never will be. It took about two years for the women to forgive me about the piece in the paper. First Missis Carney up the road stopped me in the street and started talking as if nothing had happened. And then Missis Butler smiled at me and said Hallo and it went on from there. I am in and out of everybody's bad books like a grasshopper.

I'm not much good for talking and neither is he. I need someone to strike up a conversation and lead me on a bit. My mother was a quiet woman too, but even though we hardly spoke to each other we still didn't get on. It just goes to show what a mystery life is. He and I don't get on at all but in a funny way we wouldn't have it any other way if you take my meaning.

After our drinks, by then I was on three a day, Sheila and myself went walking. We walked out of the town where it was quieter and we climbed over a gate into a field and whooped and shouted and laughed until we could take no more. When I'm with people a strange thing happens to me. After a while I think I'm part of them and not me anymore. I get confused in the head and the more they talk the more confused I get. I tell you, thank God for a birth certificate. Sometimes it's so bad I have to excuse myself and get out of the way of people. My nerves were always at me even as a child and it hasn't got any better with age, in fact it's got worse. Sheila started telling me what to do after only three weeks together and the old tension in my back started up again. She was doing it for the best, mothering me I suppose, but it felt like she had a pillow over my face and wouldn't let me breathe. Sheila was use to bossing people around you see. She came from a family of twelve and being the eldest she had to mother the ones under her.

The funny thing was she wouldn't let you mother her back and it made me feel very helpless. I know I'm bad for talking about her like this but I can't help it. *Lipstick on your collar tells a tale on you, lipstick on your collar says you were untrue.* Do you know that song by any chance? I had Sheila's lipstick on the collar of my blouse from all her kisses. There's something very glamorous about putting colour on your lips before you go out. When I was young boys fell in love with me. I remember it well. I want it back. I use to feel great with all the boys fussing over me. It's a long time since a man looked at me in that way. I felt very lonely and sad when it stopped as if I'd lost something beautiful. It makes me feel wretched. All the women's magazines say this is the age of the older woman. What rubbish, age is a disease and that's that. I miss the boys looking at me in the streets. I never really knew what or who they were looking at but all the same it was better than nothing. As I got older I compared everything in life to nothing. No matter what rows and fights were going on I'd always say, 'Well isn't it better than nothing.'

Once you get wrinkles your goose is cooked. I hid all this from Sheila because after a couple of jars she use to give out stink about men. I thought the best thing to do was to agree with her but I was always thinking to myself. 'But aren't they better than nothing?' She didn't see things like that. She thought the world would be a far better place without them. She was very set in her ways. When we were out walking and we told each other all the news she got very edgy as if something was the matter with her. It was then I became frightened of her. I felt the same way I did when she was mothering me, sort of suffocating in broad daylight. But we did have a lot of fun together, we'd bring bottles of stout up to the fields and sandwiches and it was like turning the clock back twenty years. She put her arms around my shoulders, they felt a ton weight on top of me but I loved her and that is what matters.

'You don't mind do you?' she asked putting her head on my shoulders as well. What could I say, I didn't want to hurt her feelings. She was fifty years old when I met her, five years older than me. She had eight children but like myself they were all grown up. She said very little about her husband. Wasn't she lucky there was no piece in the paper about him. I was nearly always drunk, I know that now but at the time I thought I was just happy. After a while Sheila became too much for me. She flew into these terrible rages when she got drunk and all I wanted to do was float around the fields and grow wings.

To get away from Sheila I went to McMullans bar on the corner of Harding Street and there I met Kate. Kate was tall and thin and wore glasses. I took her to be a schoolteacher the minute I saw her, or a nurse, she would have made a fine nurse. In fact she had a part-time job in the glass factory and looked after her old mother as well.

'I'll have a whiskey and a white lemonade,' I said.

She smiled and came over to where I was sitting. 'Don't mind if I join you, do you?'

Stout is very good for your health but whiskey is the medicine for your sense of humour. In no time we were talking like we had known each other all our lives.

I believe the best thing in the world for a man is to work with other men. It gives you a sense of yourself. It makes shape where there's only shite. The world is a whole other place when you've got others to back you up. I met this man in the pub and we got talking. We teamed up and split the spoils down the middle. We did one house every two weeks so as not to draw attention to ourselves. We got money and silver and the odd bit of clothing. People don't like parting with their money. Women are the worst.

Jerry had to give one woman a taste of his pecker before she'd tell us where the money was. She begged him for more. Piss the money she said, just screw me. She was eighty-five years old, one hardy bitch. She said she'd leave the window open in future and we could come whenever we liked. On another occasion I had to beat this bastard up because God give me patience he wanted to hand his money onto his sons. I am a son, I said to him. I am a son and a father rolled into one. People are so stubborn, they ask for a beating and then swear blind you turned on them without due cause. I have never laid a finger on an innocent man. I believe in teamwork, it's the best way to get things done. But this is a sad story, this is, because Jerry got it in the neck. He got five years in the rat trap for his troubles. I swear to God I was sitting by the fireside with my wife when it happened. I visited him once, once is enough for any man. He said there was a great difference between us and did I know what that difference was? The poor man was demented over me having my freedom while he stewed in hell. What's the point in the two of us being behind bars, I asked him. He had no answer for that.

As I was leaving he grabbed my hand and said you're the best friend a man ever had. I believe in friendship. I went out on my own for a while and then I threw my hat at it. I realised that the only thing that mattered in this world was God. I was on my way to him, God was on his way to me. We'd meet half way down an old railway track somewhere and he'd throw his arms around me. I would forgive him and he would forgive me like two old mates. He might even cry. He would bawl. God is a bawler. The least little thing goes wrong and he's all wound up. The two world wars. The frying and baking that took place some years ago in Germany. He's hurt because he loves us all so much. But God wins, he always wins, how can I love him? After Jerry life was never the same for me. A man loses his best friend and he never recovers, that's the price of friendship. The woman was a menace and my two sons had forgotten all about me. They behaved as if they were orphans. Every so often they'd turn up on the doorstep and apologise for the long delay, apologies aren't enough. It doesn't even mean you're sorry, it only means you're learning to get your own way through the odd bit of politeness. 'You are proper sons,' I said, 'not bastard sons like some I could name and yet you treat me this way.'

I restrained myself all those years ago and what do I get for it. I get two arseholes without a backside between them. The best thing in the world to be is a man, which reminds me about the killing. The one that got away, the sacred cock-up. It was plain as the nose on my face that no one had noticed he was dead. In that case no one knew he was alive, I'm talking about another orphan here, a wanderer, a child of God. Killing is necessary. It's in the old Bible, the new one was written up for those who see things in black and white. The Church has its bread and butter to think of. I too have my bread and butter to think of. The Church and me understand each other perfectly, twin brothers you might say. The priests keep the boot on the nuns, I keep the boot on my wife. The priests love the nuns, I love my wife. That's not the point. It is beside the point. In a nutshell the bread and butter is the point. A man tortures another man, it's not personal. Far from it. A man rapes a woman, it's not personal. Far from it. The odds are he never saw her before in his life. And even if he did, say it's his wife, it's still not personal. It's only a way of keeping his hand in while he can. I've never made love to anyone, I fuck instead. The woman took it to be personal. She cried for a while and then she stopped crying. She gave up on the waterworks and about bloody time too.

On one of my expeditions I found myself in an awkward position. Two old people were sitting by the fire listening to the wireless when I arrived in. They wouldn't tell me where the money was. I had to burn the woman's hand in the fire before she'd talk. I didn't like being forced to burn her hand, it was an old hand. I pitied old people, one day I'd be old myself and I'd know all about it. I wanted to kiss the hand, not burn it. All my plans fell by the wayside one way or another. I'd no intention of ever putting my hand in another man's pocket. That wasn't part of my plans. God left me no choices. You can stick free will up your arse and spend the next year constipated. But I liked being bad. I knew I was bad. It made up for a lot of things I'd forgotten about. To remember is not important. To know is important. I know everything. I am everything. I am sacred. I know what's what. I know who's who. My name is Paddy the Irishman. My name is Cyril the lad. My name is Alan the Bandit. You can love me if you like. I don't mind. I'm a good housewife, I'm a dead man. Take it as you please. Well, well. There was only one thing I ever did that I wanted to. All the rest I was forced into.

The bloody weather gets me down. One day the sun shines the next day it's raining. The weather's unsettling. A man needs to know where he stands once and for all. This is an examination of conscience. I'm doing well. I do not lick my own arse. I do not lie to myself. I get to the point of all things in a jiffy. You can get jiffy bags in any shop that sells stationery. They hold bulky things. I'll send my prick to you in a jiffy bag. Take good care of it. Store it away in a jam-jar for a rainy day. I'm finished with it. I gave it up years ago. You may as well have it. Plant it in your back garden. Come Spring you can pack it in beside the potatoes and off to the market with you. It's a bit of me. You can have a bit of me no charge, lick me free of charge if you want to. Blow me up if you can. You can use my prick to pump up the tyres of your bicycle. Miracles will never cease. Believe in miracles and blow me up. Faith moves mountains. Christ is our King. I love the King. Kiss the King for me. The King will move mountains for you. God save the King. The woman wants me to be nice to her. I am not nice to her. God save freedom before it's too late. I can do what I like, that's a joke for you. On the whole though I am an agreeable healthy man.

Da stood by the front gate thinking of barricades, bunkers, iron gates, ten foot tall walls, steel doors, machine guns, bombs, knives and swords. I hid around the side of the house and spied on him as he chatted to some of the men passing and ignored the ones he thought were lower than himself. Barbed wire fences, wooden railings, electrically controlled fencing, thick chunky locks, land mines, hand grenades, boarded-up windows and alarm systems. Watching him I wondered does he know I'm the other man yet? Is it all ahead of me? And the other thought that struck me when it was all over was, was it me he meant to kill?

He turned as if sensing he was being watched and I pulled back and plastered myself against the wall. I lit up and took a drag the way a spy would. I took the paper and pen out of the back pocket of my jeans and wrote in hurriedly: *12.30 a m – Man seen talking to another man. Definitely hanging around front gate for something or someone.* Why would someone like my Da stand around in broad daylight apparently doing nothing?

I peered around again and there he was hugging himself, his arms sprawled across his chest, his face contorted with agony as he clicked one side of his shoe in against the other. I whipped my notebook out fast as lightning and wrote, *Meeting cancelled.* I took one last peek, he was down on his hunkers, his arms tight around himself like thick rope, his face hidden in the crook of his arms. I crept around the back of the house and when I reached the dustbin around the corner, I stood up straight and casual and whistled openly so you wouldn't see the spy in me. With all my might I hated Ma for being mad about me. A hair's breadth and I was the one found buried behind the hedge. I repeated to myself, I was born lucky, I'm full of charm, I'm not good looking but you can't have everything. I got so tense I went upstairs and wanked to see if the tension would go away but it didn't. When I came back down Da had his overcoat on and Ma was brushing it down. He stood so proud then looking over us all and checking us out as if any second he might become a king again.

We didn't know then but it was his last trip into town. Afterwards I went over and over that last time, thinking of how I should have kissed him or hugged him, instead we just did the usual stuff.

'Will you be long?' she asked.

'I might and I mightn't,' he replied.

I said nothing as usual but I gave him a cool look.

'What's he think he's lookin' at?' he said.

She turned around and put her hand behind her back, waving it about like a bunch of feathers to shoo, shoo, me into the kitchen. I could hear her fussing over him to quieten him down and when he was gone she came in saying, 'That man wears me out.' Sipping tea she talked about him in a fretting way and she leaned over and patted my arm, saying, 'Well I've still got you,' as if she really believed his days were numbered. Did she guess the king went into battle with another man like a warlord from the old days? And did she secretly admire him for giving someone else their come-uppance? But there were certain things you didn't talk about in our house, nearly everything in fact. Our eyes locked together in love for the king and we sat in silence praying for his soul.

'Are you going, our love?' she said.

'Don't love me,' I snapped at her.

'Now, now, what's up? What's the matter with my little baby,' she said, leaning over and tugging on my sleeve.

'Call me Benjamin, or better still call me nothing, like Da does,' I begged.

'He can't remember anyone's name,' she scoffed.

'That's it,' I begged. 'Forget you ever saw me.'

'Son. Son. What's the matter with you?'

Lovers come and lovers go but my little Ma will never let me go. I think I'll burst if I don't wank, but I'll pass out first because it's very good for you to say no once in a while. No. No. No, along the highway. No one will make me wank. I'll be strong as my Da. No. No. No. We won't wank. Lovers may come and lovers may go but my Ma and Da will always say no to wankety, wankety, wankety, because we're the best people in the whole world. I flicked back a wing of hair off my forehead and gave her a Kape Kool baby look, everything in working order here I assure you, her sly eyes were watching me for a new weakness.

Here's what happened between us: One day I was sitting at the table drawing an elephant and she came over, ruffled my hair and looking over my shoulder she said, 'That's very nice son.' She had never said son before and my ears pricked up as if I was in a darkened room with no light at all and my ears turned sharp as needles listening for the slightest change in sound. One day everything was the way it always was and another day there was a shift, a movement that wasn't there before. I remember how nervous I felt because it was as if I couldn't hide myself when I wanted to. When I played with the boys in the school yard one of them would end up shouting at me, 'Piss off you're a fairy.' But then they seemed to forget about me as if it was only a guessing game.

'Son,' she said in a low sweet voice pressing my head against her breast as if she was frightened it would drop off. 'You're not like the others are you?' she said ruffling my hair gently the way they do in the pictures when they're going to blackmail their lovers.

Soft and gentle and sweet as a juicy plum, her voice sang my praises as if she was at mass singing the song just before the priest changes the wafer into God. I remember looking down at my copy-book and thinking I still have the elephant's leg to draw. And I remember thinking, she wants something off me. But what is it?

In the pictures the woman goes over to the window and looks out onto a big lawn for a while before turning quietly and naming the sum of money they want to keep their trap shut. But Ma didn't go to the window, she trapped my head against her chest even tighter and said, 'You're my little boy aren't you? My very own little boy,' gloating the way she does when she thinks no one is watching and she pores over her secret post office savings account. She pushed my head away and moved three feet to the back of me. 'The bloody animals,' she snapped like a knife zipping through skin. That was the other three. She didn't like them and she pressed my head back against her breast, it felt like a ball and she swayed as if she was dancing and the ball moved with her.

'You're not like the others.' she said, lovingly and stronger now as if she was delighted. In the pictures the woman drops her eyes as if she's very sad but there's nothing she can do about it. But when I looked up at Ma a look of surprise was on her face as if I was a right godsend.

'You're your Mammy's little boy,' she whispered in my ear. The other two were Daddy's boys and I was Mammy's boy. I'd rather be a Mammy's boy then a fairy any day of the week to tell you the truth. She kissed me on the mouth then as if it were sealing the truth away inside two tombs so no one would ever know but us. I jumped up out of the chair. Suddenly I felt trapped, I stood trembling on the spot, terror sprang at me like a giant claw from the wall where I'd just been. My wrists flicked out and up, I couldn't stop it, a sudden switch like that, I couldn't stop it, my arm doesn't belong to me, take your arms back, Ma. I was growing up, every second counts, suppose it gets worse, spreads to my legs, mincing down the street, I can't stop it. Snap, just like that I lost control and my arm flew up. I looked around, I got away with it this time, but never in a crowded room, oh, oh, still free, a harsh voice like a policeman, 'Got ya' and a tight grip on the wrist so you can't wriggle away, sorry I'm in a hurry must fly, 'Bye-bye.'

PART III

The Goldfish

Swims In The Sea Gasping For Air And North Meets South

I met a hero. A man of God. A man who knew right from wrong and wrong from right. A man with a brain, two arms, two legs and a head on his shoulders. What more could I ask for? A man who knew where he was going from and coming to. A man with a sense of himself. A man with a past, a present and a future. In short, a man. I met him in a pub. I was sitting up at the bar and he came in and sat up on the stool beside me.

'Nice evening,' he said.

'Nice evening,' I agreed.

I could see we were going to get on. We talked on about this and that until finally he said to me, 'You know life's not just about yourself.'

'It's not?'

'No it's not.'

'If it's not about meself, what's it about?'

'It's about other people. It's about us, all of us.'

'Is that a fact?'

'That's a fact. You'll never be a free man until we're all free. You can't be free in a vacuum,' he said.

'Curse the freedom,' I said. 'Give me a wage packet and I'm a happy man.'

'It's not as simple as that.'

'It's not?'

'No it's not.'

He went off the topic altogether, finished his pint and away with him. I felt his presence by my side long after he was gone. The power of his intelligence never left me. He arrived back at the pub a few nights later. He wasn't a regular, I'd know a regular a mile off. He sat beside me again and looked at me friendly-like, but distant. He was not to know that this was the first test I'd set him, if he had come on strong and taken the same rights as a regular he would have aroused my suspicions right away.

He nodded, I nodded. For a while he said nothing and then he said, casual-like, 'I hear you're out of work.'

'Where did you hear that?'

'You're well known in these parts,' he said.

'I'm a regular,' I agreed.

'I'm from the North,' he said.

'You don't say,' I said. His accent would knock you flat but I was biding my time, I was checking him out slowly.

'Half the town's out of work,' I said.

'And you've got a record,' he said.

I stared straight ahead of me. In all the time I'd been coming to the pub no one had said a word to me about it. But it was so straightforward coming from him, shoulder to shoulder, that I knew it was all right. I was dealing with a man who came straight to the point. At long last I was face to face with an honest man, I relaxed.

'So I have,' I agreed cheerfully. He bought me a drink. 'You're here on holiday?'

'Bit of business to look after, I'm up and down every few weeks on business. How long is it since you worked?'

'Five years.' I said. 'I get odd jobs, a week here and there. Nothing steady.'

'It's tough times,' he said.

'It is,' I agreed.

Six months of talk and checking each other over went by.

Then one evening he said to me, 'Ever think of doing something for your country?'

'No,' I said.

'Why not?'

'My Da fought the English,' I said. 'He hated them. He hated everything, he could see no reason for any exceptions. Prove yourself to me he use to say and then I'll believe. How can you prove yourself? You have to take a chance on people. You have to take a chance on something otherwise life's not worth living. Isn't that right?'

'I couldn't agree more,' he said.

Up to that point in time I hadn't given my country a second thought. I hated my country. Why should I think about it? I was up to my neck in troubles as it was. I slapped my glass down on the bar so hard it smashed to pieces.

'Fuck this country and fuck the people in it. Long live hell,' I roared, and stamped out of the pub. He didn't follow me. I liked that. It showed he was no arse-licker. If it was the woman she would be out licking the ground in front of me. I was dealing with real class here and I knew it. The mention of my country made me sore inside. The man had pressed on a nerve I hadn't even known was there. Instead of hate in my Da's eyes I could see a sadness for the first time. I tried to get a good picture of him in my mind but I could only see bits of him. One eye blinking at me, a hand floating around a room I'd never seen before. His legs walking the way he use to walk, in a quick shuffle. The only trouble was there was nothing above the legs. I recognised him by the shuffling, I knew him by the one eye. I didn't recognise the hand, on thinking about it afterwards I came to the conclusion it was my mother's hand. The next day I was up bright and early and heading in the direction of the graveyard. I thought if I stood by their graves it would refresh my memory. By the time I got to the cemetery I found I didn't give a curse one way or another. And yet I was there. You can see the pickle I was in. What is a grave but clay and muck and shit and a couple of old bones. The graveyard brought me to a conclusion I'd been trying to arrive at for years; bury the dead and forget about them. But that was not what my friend believed. He argued that the past was important because it made you what you were today.

'I've had it hard,' I said.

'We've all had it hard,' he said.

'Alright, alright,' I said.

The man bothered me, no one could have had it as hard as myself. But according to my friend some had it worse, for a long time I refused to believe him. Then I had these dreams about my Da. Well not so much him as his eye. Some nights the eye was filled with sadness and stared directly at me all night. Another night it was filled with hate. It was at this point I understood my visit to the cemetery. The fact was I didn't believe he was dead at all. I was away when I got a telegram saying, *Daddy died in his sleep last night. Funeral Wednesday at five o'clock. Mother.* Between one thing and another I never made it to the funeral.

The fact is funerals piss me off. There are far too many funerals for my liking. When my mother went the same way six months later I sent a telegram back saying, *Sorry can't make it. Crippled with a liver complaint.* How do I know my family weren't pulling a fast one on me? That they weren't trying to get me to come back home? The old bastard had been retired. He was crippled with arthritis and she was killing him with her whining. He sent the telegram himself; *Daddy died last night in his sleep.* He thought he'd soft soap me into coming home to look after him. He ate politics for breakfast, dinner and tea. He had every atrocity ever committed, every battle fought, every little detail right down to the last-minute hitches at the tip of his fingers. And he said the same thing as my friend: 'We'll never be free until this country is rid of those bastards.'

After twenty years of listening to him I came to the conclusion he was a parrot. But my new friend resurrected the past for me. There was something to me after all. I was a man with a past. I felt better in myself. I was up at the crack of dawn and I was kindness itself to her. She was grateful to me, I was grateful to him.

'Don't fill me in anymore on the history of this country,' I said to him. 'Fuck facts. All I ever got was bloody facts.'

He put his hand on my shoulder. I couldn't believe it. The last time I felt a hand on my shoulder was in the woods, the day those kids framed me. I told him how they had framed me, that I had been set up by a bunch of kids.

'I believe you,' he said.

This man, my friend actually believed me. I was on top of the world. I was the happiest man alive. We got back to talking about life. He told me that without a reason for living you're in a vacuum.

'A reason? What reason is there?' I asked him.

He shrugged his shoulders and left it at that. The fact that he didn't push it any further made me think that it must be important. He wasn't trying to get one up on me. I was dealing with a serious-minded man, a philosopher of some sort. Then the strangest thing happened. This man, my friend disappeared into thin air. Kaput. Gone. I sat at the bar in the evenings waiting to feel a hand on my shoulder, or a greeting in my ear, 'Hallo Joe, Hallo Joe.' There was no hallo Joe. There was no more long talks into the night. I felt he had probably gone the same way as my Da. He was out there in the hills somewhere lying low until the war was over. What war? I didn't know, but that was how I'd begun to see things. I scanned the papers for a word about him. It went against the grain but I even looked up the death notices in the papers.

It was his absence that finally made me realise what he was up to. This man was working his arse off to free the country. No nine-to-five piece a cake job for him. Twenty-four hours a day and his life on the line. I was in the company of top brass from the IRA. This man belonged to an organisation. He had put his hand on my shoulder and thought something of me. He sat with me for hours at a time and never got sick of me. I wept buckets when he disappeared on me. At a time like that it was my way to go searching for a woman. That didn't mean I'd come up trumps every time but it kept my mind off my troubles just to be on the look out. But this time I didn't. Jerking off in some woman's crotch had about as much appeal as stepping on shit in stocking feet. I was finished with women for good an all. Tits, bum, crotch, face, stick the lot up your jumpers. You get so tired of fucking women and I was fucking well tired of everything.

Now and again she passed a remark but on the whole she put the food in front of me and kept her mouth shut. And still no word from my friend. One day the food was all wrong.

'This food's cold,' I said.

'It's meant to be,' she snapped back at me.

'This food is very cold,' I said calmly.

'Salads are meant to be cold,' she said.

'This food is very, very, cold,' I said calmly.

'What can I do about it,' she shrugged her shoulders. 'If you brought in some money we might be able to do better.'

'This food is not what I want,' I said patiently.

'There's nothing wrong with it,' she said.

'You eat it then,' I said calmly.

'I had mine earlier.'

'I said you eat it.'

'I don't want it.' She searched her apron pocket for her cigarettes.

'Right,' I said. 'You don't want it. I don't want it.' I picked the plate up and pasted the far wall with it.

She jumped up out of the chair.

'Frightened? There's no need to be,' I said.

'I'm not frightened.' She sat down again.

I picked up an empty plate and pasted the far wall with that too. I stood up and hit her across the face. She fell to the floor. I picked her up and hit her again. Then I threw her against the far wall for good measure. I think she whined. I went upstairs, got into bed and stayed there for a week. It's possible I'm a manic depressive. I've read pieces in the paper about it. The symptoms they described are my symptoms. I felt black as the ace of spades. They say that it's an imbalance of chemicals in your body. They say it's your childhood. In another piece I read they said it was the environment. And there again they said it was your nature, you are born with it. At one stage I swore to get to the bottom of it. I stole my son's library ticket and got books on psychology. My son thinks I can't read, it is what I want him to think. You will notice I did not say my beloved son. That is because he is not my beloved son. I read at least fifty books on the subject before returning the ticket to the top pocket of my son's jacket. It was still possible I was a manic depressive. After a week in bed I felt it was time to get up. It turned out that the woman wasn't too well herself. She'd slipped and fallen on her face in the kitchen, one side of her face was all bruised and her eye was swollen.

'Off to bed with you,' I said. 'Don't you worry about a thing. I'll send your breakfast up on a tray.'

I took her in my arms and held her close to me. I loved her, the poor woman was as helpless as myself. I sent her off to bed and got the boy to make the breakfast.

'Your mother fell,' I said.

He said nothing.

I looked out the window until I could look no more and then I put my coat on and left them to it.

I knew the woman and the boy were turning against me. It had happened before and I saw no reason for it not to happen again. The woman was moody and she had a streak of badness in her a surgeon couldn't operate on. That's women for you, one minute up, the next minute down, you never know where you are with them. You can see now why I turned my back on all women. You can see now why I hate them. Why would I not hate them? You can't talk to them. It makes me laugh to hear people saying we live in a civilised society. You could turn the clock back a thousand years and you wouldn't know the difference. We have made no advances. But I'm an optimist at heart, I look at it this way, we haven't gone backwards. The fact is we run on the spot twenty-four hours a day, seven days a week, fifty-two weeks of the year. God give me patience. God keep me from all harm. God preserve me. God hear my prayers. God help me to heal the woman. God give me the strength to persevere with her. The woman falls, the boy picks her up and dusts her off. I hold her in my arms to heal her. She doesn't respond one way or another. Anyone can see she's not well. Rise up Lazarus, rise up. She's not able for the hurly-burly of this world. Shite, shite and more shite, she's having me on. She'll outlive me by a hundred years. She'll stand by my graveside and kick the top soil off for good measure. Come Christmas morning she'll do a jig on it. She didn't fall. The boy hit her, he heard her calling my name in vain and gave her a clout for herself. I'm no fool, the boy worships me, I see it in his eyes. Oh God he makes me so angry. Go away boy I say to him and get that look out of your eyes, the next thing is he'll be following me around. I've seen it before, once they worship you they stick to you like glue. They hang onto every word you say, they pester you with questions. They expect you to smile at them. They expect you to notice when they're sick, well, dead and buried. They expect you to know everything. In short the boy wants to deprive me of my freedom. Well go fuck yourself son, I'll swing from the rafters first. Freedom is everything. I am a free man. You won't find my like anywhere. The boy and woman were of no importance to me. By the time I got to the front gate of the house I'd put them out of my mind.

After two years on the dole I gave up looking for work. Occasionally people I worked for before came to the door looking for me to do the odd job. But I wasn't looking for them. I couldn't. It happened or it didn't happen. They came or they didn't come. I worked or I didn't work. Every night I'd say to myself, 'Now tomorrow first thing I'll get up and try again. I'll scour the town from top to bottom for work. I'll leave the country if I have to. I'll even think up something to do.' But I couldn't, I gave up, I admit it. But it wasn't the work. I'd given up even when I was in work. I gave up when I was very young and I never got into my stride again. I didn't notice it until the work ran out. The fact is I never even got married. It happened. And then she produced this son. I knew nothing about it. And then she produced two more sons. I knew nothing about them. Every night I had the best of intentions for the following day, but I couldn't seem to do anything about them.

The years rolled by oblivious to the fact that I couldn't keep up with them. That's why I killed him, to make up for the lost years. I sacrificed him to the Gods to make up for all I'd lost in my life. I believe in sacrifice. The cruxification is all about sacrifice. I am Christ. You're listening to the man himself. If I'm not Christ I'm very like him. We're all men. We're all alike in our ways but different in our temperaments. He had more patience and perseverence than I had – that aside, we're twins. I love Christ. I love the cruxification because it's the essence of all things. The essence of all things, that sounds good but what does it mean? I've no idea, it came to me off the top of my head. A lot of things come like that but I keep them to myself. I'm a shy man. I am awkward in company. When I was younger I use to go dancing twice a week. The waltz, the foxtrot, the cha-cha, I loved dancing. To look at me you'd never think it, but my greatest ambition in life was to be a professional dancer. I had a natural rhythm and people often remarked that I'd the makings of another Fred Astaire. He was my idol, him and Ginger Rogers were the perfect couple. Oh the way they danced, oh the way they moved, they set my feet tapping just watching them. I liked picnics too, that's how I started going up to the woods. I use to bring the sandwiches with me and sit watching the clouds in the sky. I gave up dancing, I don't remember why, I suppose I realised it would never come to anything. The facts of life have to be faced up to sooner or later. I was twenty-five years old, that particular year at least I must have made a decision. Perhaps I was already worn out from living or I hadn't the money.

One evening my friend arrived back at the pub. Frank was his name, Frank Augustus Kinley. A man with a song in his heart and a brain to beat all brains. We sat up at the bar again and I went straight for the jugular.

'I read in the papers of a bombing in Dallinahatch. Was that the real thing or was it filling up space?'

'The real thing,' he said quiet and dignified as ever you'll hope to see a man.

'And was it a proper execution or a bye-the-way at the last minute?'

'A proper execution.'

'It was well thought out then?'

'It was.'

'Everything given due consideration and formally declared to be unfit for human consumption?'

'That's right.'

'I'm relieved to hear you say that,' I said. 'One last question. Was it carried out by an amateur or a true professional?'

'What do you think?'

'I think it was carried out by a true professional.'

'You're a sound man,' he said.

Frank had luck on his side. He had an unfailing belief in himself and he believed in what he was doing, that is rare, high class stuff. Dedication to a cause and that other rare commodity, obedience no matter what. That man did what he was told without questioning it, hesitating or the hope of a bribe. He did it because he believed in what he was doing. And he was not worn out from it, he was fresh as running water.

'It must be doin' you good,' I said. 'Because you look powerful on it.'

'When a man stands by what he believes in he's nothing to worry about.'

'Do you think it'd make any difference if the Brits left?'

'We could get back to ruling our own country for a start,' he said.

Frank was not shy but he was cautious. He let me do the digging for information about him and then with a casual shrug or a grin he indicated that I was on the right track. He spoke as if the two of us were bugged but you don't have to be in the IRA to carry on like that. Every man knows someone is trying to listen and watch him in an effort to catch him out.

'You have to be careful what you say in this town,' I said.

'What do you mean?' he said. Now there's careful for you.

'Well you're right about one thing,' I said.

'Yeah?' He nodded encouragement.

'A man needs a reason for living, otherwise it's all, it's all – how can I put it to you?'

'Aimless,' he suggested.

'Yes, that's right. It's all aimless.'

'You work for the establishment, or you work against it, depending on your politics,' he said.

'Well I'm doin' neither. The establishment doesn't require my services any longer. It's all machines this, machines that.'

'I agree,' he said. 'The system doesn't work.'

'We need a change,' I said. 'But what?'

'What?'

'What change?'

'Figure it out for yourself,' he said.

The man's talk excited me no end. He went on to say that society was already in the process of change and the next few years were crucial ones. What change came about now would affect Ireland for generations to come. The first thing to do, he said, was to heal the rift between North and South. It was unnatural the way things were. I didn't believe him but I loved him because when I thought it all out afterwards I realised the answer was too simple. If it was that simple we'd be all drunk with joy.

'You're a breath of fresh air around this town,' I said. 'There's so much depression floating around it gets you down. This town is in favour of the likes of you. I want you to know that,' I said.

'I don't know what you mean,' he said. Now there's careful for you.

'You're doin' something. You're up there fightin' for your family, your history and your life. You're defendin' yourself.'

'Another pint?'

'I won't say no.'

'We need revolutionaries. We need men with ideas. God knows we've enough arse-lickers to populate the world with. It comes back to our history. Don't blame the people. We had to arse-lick to survive.'

'I hope you don't mind me saying this Frank,' I said. 'But your ideas are as old as the hills, my father use to sit in the same spot you're sittin' in right now and say what you're sayin'.'

'And he was right. But the reason it's still around is that it hasn't happened yet. We have to keep on fightin' to make it happen.'

'Three cheers for a good fight,' I said, raising my glass. 'No better man than meself for a bloody good fight.'

After a while I said to him, 'What about other ideas, there's more then one way of skinnin' a goat. We could come to certain agreements.'

This was the question I'd been waiting to bring up for weeks because I was still checking him out you see. I hadn't given up on that. A nerve on his cheek twitched, I'd finally reached him.

'You can't start something and let it drop,' he said. 'It takes on a life of its own. Besides,' he said, 'would you trust the English enough to talk to them?'

'Me? I don't trust my own Missis. I'm hardly likely to trust strangers,' I said.

I realised then that he was as trapped as I was and for all his big talk we were just two slaves having a drink together. But having gone so far myself I worried that I might have blown my cover. People don't trust an intelligent man as much as they do a stupid one. An intelligent man may change his mind, a stupid man has no mind to change. And you can bend a stupid man quicker to your way of thinking and that makes him more popular all around. But when Frank disappeared again I didn't fret about him, I knew he would come back to me.

Ma Watches

The Big Fish Falling For The Bait

What the women have is words, Ma said. Words can be strung together like beads on a necklace, rearranged and made into a bracelet. Half strung, quarter strung, bangles, beads, necklaces and rings. Sentences become presents. Presents passed over back walls, outside the front gates, on the streets. And if you were having a row with a neighbour you shut up and gave her no more presents. So even without money there was a way to keep your self respect, as long as the words were your own words, rearranged in your own way. And the women when speaking threw their arms out to express themselves better and show off the sparkling bracelets on their arms. But our story-talking collapsed with Grannie's mother Rachel. Up till then the women had triumphed effortlessly over their surroundings with tragic stories that held listeners spellbound. And the women, their mouths dried up from the talk, their tongues swollen, fell into bed delirious with joy while the men sat around planning and gambling and selling bits and pieces to keep the family going. Grannie's mother found a provider easily enough. Men are two a penny, she boasted to the other women. Perhaps she liked his quiff, the flat shape of his chest, or the way he said hallo to her. A thousand delicacies, only a quarter remembered now.

And when the first raindrops fell on the abandoned wasteland, Rachel said, the women expelled the mess of blood and bone and held the small pointed faces up to their arid dry breasts. Sometimes the women got down on their hunkers over a hole in the earth and expelled the mess of blood and bone and sharp pointed faces straight down into it. Then they kicked the dust back over the grave with their feet and continued on. I saw ten thousand women, Rachel said, crawling out of the gravesides on their hands and knees with hunger. They beat each other up to get out that gate in one piece. This was no orderly line of women, oh no, they squashed each other like green grapes into the ground and crawled over the dead to get out the gate. Hunger, Rachel said, hunger. They dropped the babies into the graves and ne'er a one could remember which grave it was afterwards for a starving body blots out everything but its own hunger. And it gets bigger day by day, it's not the sort of thing you can smooth-talk or satisfy in some other part of you. One day you become hunger itself, you're no longer human, you're the very essence that drove you out of the graveyard. I crushed two women's heads beneath my own knee-cap to get out that gate. I remember their faces looking up, pleading with me just as my knee-cap was driving down on them. Heroes walk with arms extended outwards to praise the glory of life but arms are soon filled, Rachel said. I saw them lying in ditches under the bridges, corpses by morning. Dogs buried the bones and not even a child could find them. Yes, yes, Rachel shouted excitedly, young son's lips brushing across his father's cheeks like a jaded dream, don't you know well. Now help me into bed before I turn into words, before I turn into the sound of words. In the name of God when will I become a vase filled with rain on the shelf? And then she said, what happened? For God's sake will someone tell me what really happened?

When I finished washing the dishes I rinsed the cloth out and put it on the line out the back. It was a good day for drying so when I came back in I went upstairs and collected all the old shirts and socks for washing. Then I came back down and boiled up another kettle of water, all the time thinking you should have thought of them in the first place and saved having to boil another kettle. I turned the cold tap on and watched it running for a while until I felt better. I couldn't stop giving out to myself. Nothing I seemed to do was right and even when I did something right I couldn't say to myself, 'Well, that was well done.' What I did was I ignored it and waited until I did something wrong again.

I gave up drinking altogether because I couldn't seem to stop at one or two. As well as that the housekeeping money ran out and he started getting at me for not managing it better. Little did he know where it was going. I was drunk every day of the week at one stage. He was away so he never found out about it. When I woke up in the morning I could see a warm rosy glass of whiskey waiting on the table for me. My mouth use to water at the thought and then I'd become aware of this knuckle knocking on my forehead and my mouth dry as a bone and my tongue swollen. I can't say I felt terrible because I've often felt worse with not a drop taken. So there you go, the devil you know is better than the devil you don't know. There was a voice inside me, well there were a lot of voices all talking away nineteen to the dozen, but this particular voice was a bit different. This person, this voice, hated me. No matter what I did there was no pleasing her. Though I couldn't actually see her I could sense things about her, for instance she'd never laugh or smile or want to do anything that was good for her. She seemed to hate everybody, especially me.

I think there is such a thing as spirits who for one reason or another can't rest in the next world. Well one of them took up lodgings in my head. The hangovers didn't put me off drinking. Not even the looks of pity when I was thrown out onto the street for making a nuisance of myself. I don't remember it but the judge said I did. Mister Burke the barman, I think he's the manager, he's certainly not the owner, stood up on the stand and said I had turned over two tables in the pub and broken about twelve glasses into the bargain. Good enough for him, they charge enough to allow for a table to be turned over now and again. Nail the tables down if they're that bloody worried about them. The judge let me go on account of *him* being inside at the time. That was a lie, he was in digs down the country. But never mind I got off with it and that's the main thing. It did give me a fright though, I could see where I was going, downwards into the gutter with all the other slopheaps. If you can manage to keep a roof over your head at all you're alright. I didn't want to end up being a bag-lady. Well I took myself off to another pub. After a year of it the steam went out of it. It was more habit than anything else. The excitement had worn thin, a bit like a drink a man is, in the beginning it'll save your life and at the end it won't let go of you. I'd never go home until I'd sobered up. I didn't want the boy to get the wrong end of the stick. At his age they're very gloomy. They sit around waiting for World War Three to arrive on their doorstep. He'd no energy and he spent most of the day looking at himself in the mirror. You can't be too careful with children, if he saw me with a drop taken he'd be sure to add it to his list of reasons for killing himself. Aren't they always thinking about killing themselves at that age? Dick and Andy were exactly the same. They play a kind of game with themselves, 'Will I go on, will I not go on?' It makes them feel they are daredevils and passes the time for them. Howanever he was not going to see his mother drunk and that was that. When the court case came up I poo-pooed it all away as a big mistake. 'What can you expect from barmen,' I said. 'They're all contrary bastards with no home to go to.'

Ben seemed to take a shine to me from an early age. I was very surprised by the whole thing. He was very enthusiastic about me, always buying me sweets and such like. Well it turned out later he was stealing them, but howanever, they ended up in my apron pocket. Naturally I was flattered, who wouldn't be. I like the boy. He's good to me. Often when they're safely out of the way I say to myself, But what is a mother? because I don't feel any different to when I was a young girl. I felt older but no different. He must see something I don't see. I can't say I didn't enjoy bingeing because I did. I was very proud of the friends I made, all true-blue women and they loved me just like Ben did.

It was a wonderful surprise to find out that people liked me.

He's the popular one around here. He knows everyone and everyone knows him. You'd think after the piece in the paper they'd turn against him. Not a bit of it, he was as popular as ever. I suppose they made excuses for him. It was a damn sight more than they did for me. I don't remember how many I drink, drank a day because of course it's all behind me now. I started at one and ended up with? Is this all in my head? Is this happening to me? It couldn't be happening to me. I won't let it happen. I won't, I won't, I won't. Children are liars aren't they. Where was I? *On top of old smokey all covered in snow*. What comes after that? Who knows? God knows? The children know? Will I be safe here? No, no, there's nowhere safe. I'll just have a little snifter. I can't go on without a little snifter. Oh just a teeney, weeney drop on my tongue. Excuse me a minute. Ah there now. Ah that's lovely, that's more like it. I'm better, I'm much better. I can go on a while longer. I can, what a wonderful life I've had. I hear them at it everywhere I go, they haven't a bloody clue. I'm beginning to sound like him. He likes to tell the world and its mother how to live. They come to him for advice. To him! You'd know about these things Joe, they say to him. Well he goes on for hours doling it out like medicine drops. The sun shines out of his arse as far as they're concerned.

I can't imagine what it's like not to be married. It must be awful. People bother you when you're on your own. They keep pushing you into doing something with yourself, or they make use of you seeing as you've no children to look after. Between babysitting and looking after an old mother, or some woman down the road sure you might as well get married. Three cheers for marriage, it keeps you out of harm's way. Ben's a sweetie, a little old darling. He would do anything for me. I said to him one day, I said, I haven't a penny in my purse darlin' and that father of yours is due home. I started crying into my apron though to tell you the truth I didn't feel like crying. I was more angry than sad if you know what I mean, but you can't be angry can you. They'd flay you alive for it. You know why, because it's powerful stuff that's why. He was at me for years to give it up. Every time I got angry over something he'd say, 'You lookin' for a fight, I'll give you one.' But I never said I was looking for a fight off him. Men don't like it in a woman because it's powerful stuff, well it's not half as powerful as the queer stuff is. Anyway I was crying into my apron and Ben says, 'Don't cry Mammy I'll get it for you.' And off he goes into the town.

Well to tell you the truth I forgot all about the money and him what with the cleaning and sorting out to be done. He arrives back close to teatime and lo and behold there in the palm of his hand are two ten pound notes winking up at me.

'Where did you get them?' I said.

'Ask no questions, get no lies,' he said stuffing them into my apron pocket. Well if that's not love for you, what is? He was only ten years old at the time but he kept me out of trouble. He's the light of my life. He only has to see a tear in my eye and he's off out looking for a few pounds for me. I'm glad there was no daughter, sure aren't they too close to you. And if you cried wouldn't they know bloody well, worse still wouldn't they be crying themselves and doing you out of your few bob. Sons are the best, they don't really understand you. There's nothing worse than being understood. Sure isn't that what closeness is all about, isn't it now. *Show me the way to go home, I'm tired and I want to go to bed.* I gave up drink, when did I give it up? *Janey Mac, me shirt is black what'll I wear for Sunday?* None of them know I take a drop. There's no sympathy for a drunken woman. A drunken man now, ah well the poor lad can't help himself. There's justice for you, there's no bloody justice unless you pay for it. Then you can buy it by the bagful, oh the justice is full of understanding if you're lining his pockets. I'm sounding like *him* again. He's one bitter man. I've come across bitter men in my time but he takes the biscuit.

'The working class,' he says as if he was crunching glass. There's some man he meets in the pub and he fills him up with rubbish. He comes home here and the bitterness and anger he pumps out of himself, sitting right here where I'm sitting now, spewing it out, 'his country this . . . his country that.' 'And the working classes are downtrodden,' he says, 'and they sit on their arses and do fuck all about it.' And that's suppose to be a speech! I feel sorry for him. This other man twists him around his little finger and I'm left having to listen to him throwing up the left-overs.

'I'm becoming politically aware after all these years,' he says to me.

'You haven't a stitch in your trousers and you let that man use you like that.'

'Isn't he trying to put a stitch back in all our trousers?' he said.

'He's looking after himself,' I said.

'And the rest of us,' he said.

'If the rest of us get anything out of it it'll be an accident.'

Here I was talking to a man who used his fists to get the better of me but when I saw he was trapped in his own fighting, that it wasn't a one-off row, then I was sorry for him, he was more to be pitied than feared. Here's to you. Up yours. Three cheers. A little snifter to keep me going. Tell me nothing. I don't want to know. What can I do? Sure aren't we all fighting with ourselves. There's a knack in getting control of yourself. What is it? I am. I am not. I will. I will not. I do. I do not. I don't care. Well with not caring came the freedom to be myself. I had a look in the mirror, I really looked. I was mangled, a heap of a mess of a thing you'd hardly call a woman. But I felt looking at myself instead of avoiding was a step in the right direction.

In the beginning I was no different from anybody else. I just couldn't make it. I am a weak woman. I do not like myself. I was never loved. I was never wanted. I will never be loved. I will never be wanted. But I must get to the end of it. I must not cut my wrists, slit my throat, throw myself in a river, throw myself off a high-rise building. Take pills, or take pills and drink together. Instead I must die of natural causes because I am a natural woman. And I must hide all this from my son. This is me, or something like me. This is him or something like him. The boy must not see his mother has given in. I go on for my son. Without him what am I? I am an ugly woman. It is impossible to like me. It's all right I know it. I spent my life pretending and I know I'm not alone. Not that I care one whit. I am behind him all the way. He is my husband and I'll never leave him. Whatever he says goes. I love him. I hope he never dies. God bless you love. Take good care of yourself. Someday I'll tell you I love you. I'll say it straight to your face. I love you, I'll say. And you'll say back to me, I love you too. We love each other. I'm parched with the thirst. I loved to sit in a field and suck grass. I loved to watch the clouds bobbing about over my head. I loved to pick daisies and make daisychains with them and remember my young days. A long hot summer's day and nobody at me. Was it better in those days? I think it was, and the people were friendlier too. I love to think back to what I might have been. Ah sure you'd no chance in the old days. But I had, I had. What was it? What was the chance I had? It's always there in the back of my mind. You got your chance and you passed it up. What did I pass up? Bad sess to the lot of you, I can't remember. Ah there, that's better, that's it. I feel nothing. Before you know where you are life has turned sour on you, that's a trick. Take it away and give me another drinkee, that's what I say. 'Tell you a secret, tell you a secret, tell you a secret before you go to bed.' What secret? 'Tell you a secret, tell you a secret before you go to bed.' I saw a little dark-haired girl calling out to me like that, 'Tell you a secret,' she sang, 'Tell you a secret before you go to bed.' Is my son really a daughter? I had a little girl after all. Ben, Ben it's Bernadette. Isn't that it? Oh Bernadette come to Mammy. Mammy wants to talk to her little girl. Saint Bernadette, she saw our Lady didn't she? Your Mammy needs her medicine before she goes to sleep. If only I could rest awhile. If I had a girl I'd strangle her with my bare hands. I'd twist her neck 'til I heard it crack. Shut up, I'd scream. Shut up bitch and let your Mammy rest awhile.

I knew before he'd done it that he was about to do it. I knew. I knew. I knew. There now. There now. I've said it. But I knew by him. I knew. Keep away, I said to myself that very night, he's looking to rip someone apart. I could see it in him. Run Daddyo, run like hell while you can. Poor Daddyo, he gave me a son. Or a daughter. He gave me something anyway. 'Now don't tell me I never did a thing for you,' he said. My own little messenger boy. Peekaboo come to Mammy. Mammy needs a message, I click my fingers at him, messenger boy. Come here immediately. Didn't you hear me call you? I'll throw you out onto the street if you're not careful. That's the best thing about kids, they have to do what you tell them because you can always starve them if they don't. *Poor Oul dicey Reilly he has taken to the sup, poor Oul dicey Reilly he just couldn't give it up.*

Your poor Daddy didn't know what he was doing. God bless him he's innocent. They've hanged an innocent. They haven't hanged him. Why not? What's keeping them? The poor man didn't know what he was doing. I tell you he was innocent as the day is long. They nicknamed him the Butcher Crawford. The Butcher, my husband, my lovely husband. I'm not saying he didn't lose his temper. But he's no butcher. Ah well! Thumbs up and what have you. I must write to him some time.

The Melting Pot

The queen waves her magic wand in the air and poof like magic she makes the king happy as Larry. He smiles as if someone is taking a photograph of him, all teeth and big eyes and best side out if you please. Bargain-hunters keep out, my Ma and Da are not up for sale. I'm fierce that way, my Ma and Da are mine forever because the three of us make one just like the three divine persons in the one God. I love them so much that when I close my hand tightly they are inside my fist squealing to be let out. Love was everywhere like the buttercups of May, dancing on our tongues, patting our heads and then the full shilling, a big happy smile. The queen had it in her power to make us happy or sad and the king stared at her with awe and reverence, for sometimes he thought she was the Virgin Mary. The luminous blue queen with her hands outstretched as if saying, 'There you go now boys. Isn't it a grand day.'

The king was afraid to go against her in case she condemned him to hell. His eyes grew tired and bloodshot from keeping guard against the monsters that are after you wherever you go. It was his duty to keep us from all harm and he stayed up all night while we slept and dreamt our way through the black dark. 'God bless you,' she'd say, as she went on up to bed and he raised his eyes to heaven, thanking his lucky stars for a blessing instead of a curse. Deep in prayer she turned trance-like as he called her for something and he said, 'It's nothing,' knowing at that second she was in touch with holiness and wasn't to be disturbed. I bowed to her as she went by and inside I recited a Hail Mary. Da called my name softly, 'Ben,' he called just to say he was my Da and I was his son.

'Son don't forget to clean your shoes for the mornin'.'

'I won't forget Daddy,' I said and though it was late at night and he was on duty he took time off to say, 'Take care son, don't let the fleas bite.'

'I will Daddy.'

But sometimes I was trapped inside my dream and couldn't get out, how could I tell him when I was fast asleep?

He shoved my Ma around to win her love but I won hands down with my charm and he didn't like it one little bit. And I won it with my one quarter inch that I grew in the two months of my summer holiday. I was almost up to Ma's shoulder so she needn't be ashamed of having a squirt around her. But my finger nails are sensational, long and shapely like a girl's. I wouldn't have minded some clear nail varnish on them but I didn't want to get caught. And my hair is something else again, it's long and glossy and thick and it drives him wild. He liked short back and sides because it was more manly looking. But my legs aren't worth talking about and as for my chest well I was all rib cage and hardly any skin at all. My face is long and narrow and when I'm serious I'm very gloomy-looking. I got no pimples though which is something don't you think? Some of the lads in school were covered in them and they made me sick just to look at them. What I got was a rash all over my chest and down my arms. It was red and scalded-looking as if I had burnt myself. My girlfriend came with me to the doctor because she was convinced I couldn't speak up for myself. The doctor gave me antibiotics and said the rash was from nervous tension. It cleared up for a while and then came again.

Ma and me never actually held hands though we wanted to very badly. I think it's just convention because it seems strange to me – when it wasn't so long ago we held hands tightly as we went from shop to shop. I was smaller then, if that's possible. Anyway after the doctor we headed for the coffee shop on the main street to cheer ourselves up. I had one sticky bun with jam in the middle and a cream bun. Sweet things make me feel better. I could eat chocolate and sweet things until they come out of my ears. We were very happy together, it was like one long honeymoon. The only reason we didn't get married was because he wouldn't divorce her. If he divorced her we'd have married in Gretna Green the very next day. So what was I to do? I am not ashamed of what I did, I am only sorry my plans didn't turn out the way I wanted them to. To this day I'm still puzzled over what happened. You know that line in a song, I can't think of the name of the song but it goes like this, *Spread your tiny wings and fly away*. You can dedicate that to my Ma because that's just what she did. I hadn't planned on her betraying our love and leaving me in the lurch. I thought she would be honoured to have me for keeps. I thought I was doing her a big favour but it looks like she was only using me after all.

Around that time I stopped thinking of them as a king and queen and all that stuff. I loved them and all but I couldn't think about them in the same way anymore. Did that have anything to do with her betraying me? I'm sure she saw it in my eyes that I was hard put to see them as extraordinary and blue blood and all that. One day I saw the whole world as an extraordinary wonderland and then it all changed for me. Maybe she saw the change in my eyes and fell out of love with me. Was the way I saw them my charm? Does charm disappear overnight or are you charming all your life? I searched the mirror for my charm but all I saw was the most ordinary-looking boy ever.

Here's a song for you to see if I still have charm: Does my Da want to munch me like liquorice sweets and kiss my hand like the Virgin Mary is a big queen and only the best for you? Or lick me all over like Mary and Jesus holding hands out walking, for he said, 'It's a shame to stay in on a day like this Mary. Put your cloak on and we'll take in the air and rub dust on our heels in memory of a shower of tinkers that did it to me.'

She left her big black pot full of stew brewing on its own over the low light, and covered her shoulders in blue prayers so glorious and stitched together in a symphony of summer lace and rippling in the breeze where silence is love, saying, 'Never mind son. You just be yourself. That's what matters.' But all the tinkers laughed, saying to him from behind the briars, 'We saw you Friday bleeding and look at you now. All done up to the nines. Risen up out walking with your Mother, can we kiss you? Can we?' And he said, out walking, 'Perhaps my lips, just one kiss for the first night, perhaps go on, kiss me. But do none of you ever listen to anything?' And Mary fans him with her body to cool his temper for if a man is crucified the least you can do is wash your ears.

'I'm all iron and metal today,' Jesus said. 'It's them nails again. I wish I was born in a circus not a stable. The stable was no joke, you know,' he said to Mary. 'It was a bloody curse all round.'

The stable was our shed around the back of the house where Da kept old things. Da was always routing around the stable and Jesus was so fed up with him, he said, 'Sit down and shut up. You're messin' up the straw on us.' He told Da off and Da blushed scarlet and sat and pressed his face down into his knees and he turned to Ma and said, 'It's up to yourself really dear.' And Ma's eyes twitched nervously like chattering birds at that and she said in a high-pitched voice, 'Oh it couldn't possibly be up to me.'

Perhaps if I were to faint inside or curl up on Mary's lap and be covered in the Mass all over so they said on the cross he wept and wept and the two robbers were mortified for a fellow crying. Oh they hit him all over the roads like rubber and Pontius said, 'Go away you fool. Go away quick or you'll force me into it.' And Jesus said, 'Can I? Can I do that to you?' And Pontius said again, 'Buzz off will you because they are smelling blood and smelling it nothing will satisfy.'

Pontius is not my uncle, I thought and I hid my face under a shadow like a long fingernail and listened on. And all the women were mad about him and they sang, *Oh Jesus is my love*, and the men were so jealous some said that's why they did it to him. So when they took Jesus down off the cross the women bound him in cloth and covered him with their perfume so the men wouldn't smell the blood. Then they brought him to a cave deep in the ground and looked after him for three whole days.

I was in the hall. I felt a change in the house, then tensions slipping, shifting like drifts of invisible sand. Their voices rising and falling in the kitchen like claps of thunder, harsh clanging voices like the sound of iron gates shutting and opening, opening and shutting. I heard her face being cracked by Da, now her mumbled sounds of protest, now a cry, now silence. My position was now suddenly very clear to me, I was no more safe at home than I was in the streets. I hopped it.

She didn't expect him to cave in so easily. He glowered kicking out as if he was being electrocuted, then glancing over at the clock, 'Is life nearly over yet?' Like a lamb to the slaughter, she thought, so he was feeling that bad. THAT BAD. That Bad. FEEEEELING TERRRRRRIBBBBBLE. Oh Goodee goody, gum drops. Delighted for you, he was in bits, he was in need of her. Here, here take my hand, go on don't give it another thought, take it, take it, move a bit closer dear, oh what a pity you didn't quite make it, poor pet, oh well don't give up. Ooooooops missed again. He was on his knees now begging her for help. Oh he needs me, he needs me. She stretched and yawned and hummed aloud, *If I ruled the world, every day would be the first day of Spring.* And she thought for the first time that it wasn't easy to be decent and treat another person with respect. It took courage and faith in mankind. It was in fact impossible, she thought briskly, simply impossible to be decent. 'Snap out of it Joe,' she barked across the room. 'You've been sitting in that chair for days now.'

He jumped as if the remark was a whip-lash across his face. He was no more than a machine, that with a bit of oiling, a twish here and there of his nuts and bolts and he'd be back in working order, providing for her. He was winded. She was right he was a burden on everyone.

'You're in great form,' he said accusingly. 'What's up with you?'

'Nothing,' she said. 'It's the weather, sunshine always puts me in good form.'

'Some form,' he sniggered. 'Singin'.'

Da warned me to tell the truth. Am I telling the truth? He said to put it down so that people would look back in a hundred years time and see the truth staring them in the face. But once I couldn't see them as a king and queen anymore I kept getting confused. What if he wasn't a king and what if she wasn't a queen? What then? Who were they? Where will I find the truth? I got so confused and tense when I concentrated on the word truth that I went down to Markey's Supermarket and nicked forty cigarettes and then I went and stood on my favourite patch for the rest of the day and smoked my head off.

Soon I reached the point where I had to suck off other men for a pint. And I could think of nothing but money. Morning, noon and night it was money, money, money. I was sick of it. A man needs money and he needs a challenge to keep him on his feet. He needs a bit of excitement to keep the ball on the hop. I was sick of crawling through windows late at night to get my dues. Was it depression that killed the excitement? Howanever I needed a new way of living. A whole new approach to keep me ticking over day by day. I began hating the woman again. Everywhere I went there she was in all shapes and sizes. The bitches were everywhere looking for a good thrashing. I'm your man to put them in their place. I am everything. I know everything. I planned nothing, if you plan something it takes the excitement out of it. The warm feeling inside dies out by the time you're finished thinking about it. Do it or don't do it, that's my motto. I tell you here and now I love fighting. I found a woman on her way home one night and I got her up the back lane beside Cheevers Street and I fucked her and beat her up. She was a total stranger and yet I tell you as I was letting her have it I felt love for her. 'I love you,' I whispered to her. 'I love you my little hen, my little chicken nooky.' She was out cold at the time which is bloody typical.

I was filled with excitement for days afterwards. I hit the headlines again. Front page news. Woman found beaten up. Nothing about the love or the time and effort that went into it. And I could have been caught, I could have been found out. What about me? Where do I come into all this, I'm a fucking assailant, that's what they called me. What's that suppose to mean. Nothing about me feeling terrible, oh no. It was all about her and God love her and all that thrash. God love me. Did I ever hear anyone saying, God love me? It was fuck you son you're a bloody nuisance. The papers are a cod. All the same I felt contented again. I was happy as Larry, life's worth living when you're happy. I felt good in myself, I felt important. I had set out to achieve something and by God I had done it. It was proof positive I wasn't useless. A man is his own judge as to how he is. He's the one that knows himself. I was on page three the following week. They said the girl was in a stable condition. God bless her, I meant her no harm.

I wish I could pack my bags and leave myself behind. But you can't can you? You have to stay with yourself for life. My blood boils thinking of it. Who had the nerve to do that to me. I was given no choice. I was told what to do. Live with yourself, that was the order from above. I've been put in an impossible situation. I hadn't even got around to sucking my thumb when I was ruined. God spits on the innocent. He hates babies, they give him the creeps. After all he's a man, what does a man want a baby for. He doesn't want a baby, that's it in a nutshell. God threw me down here to be rid of me and expected my father to pick up the tab. My father was fighting mad over it, 'Go back where you came from,' he use to say. It's the same all over the world, who is the arsehole in the sky to tell us what to do? Well life has its rhythms, one day I was happy and the next I was sad. I'm fairly certain now I'm a manic depressive. Who wouldn't be in my boots. Sadness is something there's no accounting for. I wept for the world and its mother. I tell you it's well nigh impossible to live. You say hallo to someone and they look at you as if you've two heads. We are not friendly anymore. Our next door neighbour has become our enemy. Here and now I want to say, I love everyone. There are no exceptions. The crummiest bastard in the world has my love and my gratitude. I am glad he's alive, no matter what he's done it's all right with me. Let him live. Let him breathe. Heil Hitler. I love Hitler. He's my next door neighbour. The poor man was misunderstood. He made a mistake, he felt rotten, he didn't know what he was doing. He probably woke up one morning, had a look out the window and said, 'What in the name of Jesus is goin' on out there?'

And they did it all in his name. Balls to that, they did it for themselves. The man was a weed for Christ's sake. All the same, all the same, let him live on in all our memories. I am a generous man. I am a mild-mannered, even-tempered man. I am big-hearted and happy, if things had worked out for me I might have been an archbishop. Religion is a club for the boys. We are God. God is us. Whenever a bishop opens his mouth he knows it's God speaking. He has money, a car, holidays and the world at his feet. The Pope is a great man. He's the best actor in the world, there's no one to touch him. All this kiss me hand and I love you, I love you, in that accent of his. Ah kiss me arse. The saga of the Popes is a sorry one. They get to the top of the heap and they don't want to die.

The woman and me hate each other's guts. There is no reason in the wide world why we should and yet we do. I say to the woman I love you and the next minute I hate her. I say to the woman I hate you and the next minute I love her. I am in torment. I was born tormented. You can see there's no let up, no change of direction or fresh challenge on the horizon. I'm bored to tears. You'd never think to look at me that I was bored. Well I am. I have tried everything and done nothing. I look like a farmer, I'm rugged and bulky-looking. You'd think I'd grown up with the spuds growing under my feet. But you can't tell anything by looking at someone. Another thing about me is that I look as if I could withstand anything. Well looking is one thing, as they say in all the best comics. Comics should replace the Bible. I got more fun out of reading comics than anything else.

My mother God rest her soul was a fine lump of a woman. I take after her. I wish I could remember some of the things she said to me. Was my mother a mute? I expect she was. Let's say she didn't like talking. Let's say she didn't like talking to me. Now you see why I didn't go to her funeral. Now you see what I had to put up with. You push people too far and what do you expect them to do. No sir, up she rises, yes sir down she goes. Ready sir, finger on trigger. No sir, yes sir, boom, boom. I will call my friend Sylvester. I remain loyal to him in spite of everything. To rat on a mate, a brother in arms is to lick the gutter dry. I go to my grave with sealed lips. Sylvester continued to meet me in the pub. He asked after your mother. He asked after you. He spoke of you as if you were his own son. He said some day we would be all free and you will have a job to go to. His own son was two years older than you.

'You have a fine family,' he said. 'A family you can be proud of.'

My family is my treasure chest. My heart is always with you and your mother and Dick and Andy. I dream of the day when we'll all be together again, it'll be just like old times. We'll go on a picnic. We'll sit by the fire of a winter evening and talk of the old days. We'll draw on our memories the same way your mother draws on her cigarettes. We'll make sandwiches at two in the morning and watch the sun rise up over the hills from the back bedroom window. Tell your mother it'll be a second honeymoon. Tell her my case is up for appeal and I'll be coming home to her soon. Your mother never writes to me, you'd think I was dead the way she carries on. She'll be sorry, tell her I'll have her knee-capped if she doesn't put pen to paper soon. They disowned me in public because I had a prison record. They like you to have a clean slate when you start out so you can call yourself a political prisoner. But in private it was another matter, in private I'm a hero. If they were to own up to me they would be told the whole organisation was full of common criminals. A slur on the face of the IRA wouldn't do son. I don't mind being a common criminal. It has its advantages. People expect little from you. And they don't like you. You could say the same thing about a rich man. The next time you see a rich man kiss him for me, we're blood brothers.

One day Sylvester said to me, 'Would you like a job Joe? Would you like to help free your country from English pigs?'

His idea was to incorporate my new-found aspirations with the practical everyday reality of living.

'Kill two birds with the one stone you mean?' I said.

I love my country. I love the lush green grass and the craggy face of the mountains. I tell you son a blood-bath is no bad thing. It clears away the tension in the air. People come to appreciate life in a new way after a blood-bath. You look at any war and its after-effects. It's like washing your eyes out, you can see clearly with the tension gone. Romance is in the air in earnest, love can flow again. There is a point in time when we can stand it no longer when we must do something. My time had come. I rose up out of the ashes and did what I had to do. I had never killed anyone before. My heart thumped with excitement at the thought of it. You'd think I was on drugs the way I felt. I kissed your mother, I even kissed you. I cut the grass for the widow woman down the road, what's her name, Missis Bannon. I washed her kitchen walls down for her. The poor woman was starved for human company as much as anything else. I had dinner in her house and then I came home and had another dinner. It was akin to climbing Mount Everest. All that stuff you see in the papers about regretting this or that killing but it was necessary and so on, it's all bullshit son. It's a wonderful experience. Everyone should kill someone at least once. It clears your head. It makes you feel ten feet tall. Killing is power son, let no one tell you any different.

When the last breath had gone out of him I felt calm. Civilisation has left us starved for what comes most naturally to us. Don't join the crowds of mortified dead, son, ashamed of what they were and trying hard to be proud of what they've become, snivelling paupers too cowardly to fight their corner. Which reminds me of my lump, but that's another story. When Sylvester offered me the job I himmed and hawed until all the cards were on the table.

'Well it's the best offer I've had all week,' I said. 'All year', I added under my breath.

'You're interested then?'

We sat drinking side by side at the bar talking about religion, jam-jar ethics I called it. We discussed politics and he spoke of the pain in his heart at the division in our Isles. He said he wouldn't be happy until Ireland was united and the British pigs were stiffs safely buried under the soil. He said there was one particular chap in the organisation, a real gorilla who had been feeding information to the pigs for over a year. He came down south regularly, he said, as a matter of fact he has a cousin he stays with in this very town. So you see where religion and politics was leading us son. It was leading us to the fact of the matter; the talker had to be stopped.

'The world's full of talkers,' I said. 'Big blabbers who don't know when to shut up.'

'You understand then?'

'Sure I do,' I said.

'It's not just a question of warning him off,' he said. 'He's been warned off before.'

'Don't say another word,' I said. 'I take your meaning.'

When we parted company he shook my hand warmly. 'You'll never regret this Joe. I'll let you know the arrangements later.'

'You take good care of yourself,' I said. 'You hear me now.'

A strange thing happened after that night. As the days wore on I began to feel sorry for the poor bugger. I knew what it was to be desperate, God knows what led the man to betray the organisation and think he'd get away with it. Whatever it was, the poor bastard obviously felt cornered. But to think he could pull a fast one on the hand that fed him. It didn't add up. The gorilla was either mad or suicidal. But if he was mad the pigs wouldn't take any notice of him. I went into the church and lit a candle to the Sacred Heart for the poor bugger. You see son the poor man wanted to die and I was the one chosen to carry out his wishes. Life is sacred and I intended to give him a proper send off. I've seen men blow the shit out of someone and not care tuppence for it. They are the psychotics you read about in all the textbooks on psychiatry. The darlings of all the armies in the world, zombies who die at ten years old and hang about until someone thinks to bury them. I can't stand them. Just being in their company is enough to cheapen your soul. There is something I've been meaning to tell you for a long time son. Your mother is psychotic. All the symptoms are there. She died when she was four years old. You ask her. She can't remember anything that happened to her after that because it had no effect on her. A short life eh! Pack your bags and get out, your mother will reduce you to a farthing before she's through with you. She thinks you're a doll she got for her third birthday. Say to her life is sacred and see the blank look in her eyes at that. I am a manic depressive but I admit it. A manic depressive is someone who finds it very hard to live. Is there anything wrong with that?

I went into training for the big day. I went on a diet and walked six miles a day. I'm against jogging, running and jumping over fences. It's bad for your heart. I gave up drink. It was Lent on a grand scale, instead of cutting back I gave everything up. I felt pure and clean and once a day I slipped into the church and said a prayer to the Lord. I was undergoing a religious experience, a transformation was taking place before the eyes of the world. Every morning I got out of bed, lay on the cold floor and did twenty press-ups. What a way to start the day eh! After about three weeks of it I was puffed out altogether. Instead of thinking to myself I'll get up and do my exercises now, I'd think, 'Oh Christ I've got to get up and torture myself again today.' What's that to a man eh? It's death to him. If only Sylvester had contacted me before the rot set in I'd have been in tip-top shape but no, not a word from him. And instead of money all day long I thought of food. If only I'd had a photo of the man to keep me going but Sylvester said he'd give it to me the night before the big day. I suppose he didn't want me to brood over it. The diet fell by the wayside on the fifth week as the waiting got to me. I went around the town asking after him.

'Anyone seen Sylvester?'

'No.'

'Tall thin chap with an accent that'd crack bricks.'

'No, sorry Joe, wasn't he down here a few weeks ago?'

'He was.'

'Ah sure he'll turn up again.'

'Have a drink Joe.'

Bang went the drink of me.

'You're always in a tearin' hurry these days.'

From these snippets of conversation you can see that the whole town knew about the job and backed me all the way. There was a lot of back-clapping and jokes about my new-found friend. But underneath all the soft talk I could hear them saying, 'Get him for us Joe. Get the lousy bastard.'

They could see I'd run out of steam and were willingly giving me a helping hand. I tell you son the only difference between the man who commits the act and the one who doesn't is a limp dick.

The lump at the side of my neck remember? That friendly harmless little thing, hardly bigger than a pimple, a mate of his has sprung up on the other side of my neck. Why if something is friendly does it keep coming back? What does it want off me? Why not try another neck for variety. Why my neck? Why me?

The woman laughed and said it was probably just a cyst. She wouldn't look at it and she wouldn't look at me.

'Have you ever looked anyone in the eye?' I said.

She muttered, 'No.' This means son your mother does not know what the human eye looks like but she sure knows a lot about shoes. Naturally the lousy bitch backed me to the hilt. The first sign of trouble and she's out the door. She didn't look steady on her feet to me. What the hell's the matter with the woman? How can you go to a doctor without back-up? I stopped exercising immediately. It was plain as the lump on my neck all exercise was bad for you. I ate when and what I wanted. And I began planning some small jobs while I was waiting to hear from Sylvester. I went around the town and picked out two houses to start with. It kept my spirits up so I could plan for the future, what future you might ask? Well all you can do in this world is keep your fingers crossed and hope for the best.

I thought I would do a few houses and put enough aside to start my own business. That's power for you, standing over the workers and cracking the whip at them. I'd leave her and take the boys with me. The past is a mess but the future is a shining light. Failure gives you a bad impression of yourself. Day after day I failed to get on top of things, the work was useless, it meant nothing to me. One day I was passing the bookshop on the main street when a book in the window caught my eye. It was called *The Power of Positive Thinking*. I read it over a pint. He talked about looking on your past as experiences that you can learn from. Every time you think a negative thought you replace it with a positive one. What he said made sense, but try as I might I couldn't see myself in a new way. I felt I had gone beyond even coaxing or pleading with myself. I believed that no one could reach me, including myself, even if they wanted to. Of course this could have been my natural psychological training for the Big Day. There was always the chance someone might try to make me change my mind, or that I'd lose my nerve at the last minute. Don't think with all the waiting that it hadn't occurred to me that I might fall apart before I got my chance to prove myself. And then it clicked for me, Sylvester was testing me. He'd deliberately put me on notice to test my nerves. Had I or had I not got nerves of steel? I relaxed, the tension fell away and within seconds I was joking and laughing away nineteen to the dozen.

But all good things must come to an end. I read the book through again, it was spot-on. The excitement of it lasted a good hour after I'd finished reading it. This man believed you could change your life from right this minute, this second, now, a change could take place. I waited, I watched. I could see he hadn't met the likes of me before. I am what I am, there's no changing me. And what's wrong with me as I am? It's not me, what's wrong is I'm being squashed into the ground. How could positive thinking change that?

I am a man of many moods. At one time I thought I was a manic depressive but I see now I was wrong. All my life I've been surrounded by fuss and love. My mother couldn't see that I was a man, but she could see I was her son. Her son was different to a man. She hated men, what can you expect from a woman, it's typical. I escaped her hatred by pretending to her that I was not a man. Only then could she love me. I woke up some nights believing she was kneeling beside me choking the life out of me. I became an insomniac at the age of three. I was adept at hiding my tool from her but I needn't have bothered. On her son it was all right but on a man it was another story altogether. The long and the short of it was my mother didn't recognise me unless I dressed up as her son. If I grew up she would have been grief-stricken thinking her son had died on her.

I'm not the kind of man that goes around making other people unhappy. I remained her son so that even on her death bed she could see the miracle of her creation praying by her bedside. Everyone needs to create something in life otherwise we despair too much. The town is littered with my creations. Some days I walk slowly around the town looking into children's faces and guessing which is mine. Contraception should be banned, it's the source of all despair. We fuck and nothing comes of it. Then we despair of it. I love children. As a matter of fact I came from a big family myself. The more you have the less despair you feel. One woman collared me on the street one day and demanded money off me.

'I'm only a humble gardener,' I said. 'I've no money to give you.'

God I admired her nerve. When she threatened the law on me I wanted to fuck her again I found her so sexy.

'You won't get away with it,' she said. I grinned. Oh she was a beautiful woman.

'Go ahead,' I said, 'Bring the law down on me.'

'You never even came to see the kid,' she said.

'I didn't want to upset you. I thought it best to keep away.'

Another woman demanded I move in with her and after a long discussion about it, I said, 'But how could I trust you? We meet in a pub and you invite me back to your place for a quick fuck. I was a stranger, a total stranger. How could I trust you?'

Women are so sexy when they're mad at you. They make me want to dance again. They fill me up to the brim with joy. The madder they are, the more I grin, the madder they are at me. Just think, a day will come when one of my children will grow into a woman and stand in front of another man and fill him up with joy and I will have made it happen. Somewhere in the town a young girl is getting ready to make a man happy, does she know her father is thinking of her right this minute? Does she know her mother is a right tramp, what better way to learn that life isn't perfect than through your mother.

Far be it for me to boast but I did an excellent job on the gorilla. I've always believed in putting your back into something and giving it your all. Isn't that why we get up and fight. Sylvester had become Daniel by the time he turned up again. People can read your thoughts so I was setting them a fine old trail. I want you to know that the extermination of the gorilla was not a personal matter. The idea behind his extermination is what counts, ideas before man, or to put it another way ideas before some men; blundering, greedy shit-heaps to be exact. How is your mother? Does she still love me? Does she know I tried my best? Tell her I'm a hero. I got life as you know but sure she won't notice the time passing. I practise the waltz and the foxtrot in my cell every evening.

Daniel produced a photograph in the pub of a fair-haired man with a narrow face. It was my job. 'How much?' I said. 'Just say how much.'

Where am I? Mother, mother, they call me. You can hardly call me by that name. I say it is the wind, murmurs floating on the back of the wind, it is only wind fingering the leaves, its tongue licking the lobes of my ears. All is as before, the long thin shaft of bone, a slight movement under the moonlight and you whispering, 'Are you there?' Yes I heard you, no other sound like the sound of yours, your footsteps across the floor like soft pads of cloth . . . what? The others? Of course I hear their footsteps, I'm always alert to the slightest sound. Yet if I were to say anything personal to you, not that I would, not for an instant would I intrude upon you. Are you there? Are you there? Keep away, keep away. No trace of movement about except lying in his cot looking up, legs kicking, arms outstretched. Him? No, it did not come then did it, no it did not. He looking up at me, I looking down on him. It, it, it. In the throes of sleep a bright light hovering about, a stir of life in the empty space all around me. Cover him, uncover him. It, it. Feed it, clothe it, change its nappy. Listen for it in the dark in case it called out to me. It, it. Stir of life needing me to keep it flickering in the darkness. Walk slowly along the road with him. All heads turn, stop. Look down on him, the murmurings cawing away on the silence. Head down, stop. Stop that. Head down listening for the murmurs, somewhere the murmurs. It, it. But stir of life needing me to keep it flickering in the darkness. What? What is it? What? For God's sake, almighty Christ, red pouring blood and the stink so vile. Can you see the pouring, can you smell the stink? And the mottled skin under the moonlight too tired to paint it away? Never look another straight in the face. Up to my neck in a bog of blood, mother, mother, twisting and turning my neck, straining myself listening for something. The blood blinding me and I nearly stone deaf with the strain of trying to listen. Rooted stiff with shock. Rooted still I tell you. Pah! And the fret in the passing of time, the heartbeat thudding on and on until the what! Over. Huddled up then going on, no just that I appear to be. Fingers to beckon me forwards, now backwards. They use my lips to speak through, lips move, voice answers. Pathway of my lips, marching through the pathway of my lips without a by your leave. I scuttle from corner to corner as it overcomes me. I huddle up in a ball. Mother! And yet I'm forced to move. Forced to move in spite of all my comforts, my bones stiffen, my feet cramp and I move. Or imagine I do? Imagine, Mother! Mother! Were he to say anything to me I'd jump to attention. Stop that. Stop that. The eyeballs flitting like the wings of moths in my direction. Ah! off on a wander. To the right of me. To the left of me. Gone forever now the movement around. Two legs, two arms, a head. One side fist up. Two arms, two legs, a head, other side finger pointing. Ah! No tears, weeping all done, all done. Head turns sideways with difficulty. Legs unmoving, arms unmoving. Mother! The thinning tuft of hair and skinny thighs and your womb soundlessly weeping out the words; them days in the Grove daughter with the winding lanes and the twists and turns up into the hills and Jacob's Lane, Jacob's Lane. I running up the hillside, breathless always breathless. Clear-skinned and then the long skinny legs. Oh shag and then a laugh. What! What! Did you see my thimble anywhere, I can't find it. Head bent over the lamp late into the night. Long bony hands. Searching high and low for the thimble. It belonged to my mother was all she said. Mother! She only had to look at me and it was as if she spoke ten sentences with one glance. There now, just now, I felt a trickle of something inside me. I was sure I did, though I can't be certain. It's gone. Ah! I can suck on the thought of it for weeks. To think I might have moved. To think that. Mother! Mother! One time it lashed rain and you had no coat. Still you laughed with a queer joy at being soaked through with rain and sky and you. Then lay with no thought at all in your head. Stab of joy like bolt lightning came from the sky, through the rain, through you and passed from the tips of your fingers into the wet ground and down under. Came up again, floating on a stream, a bubble that flowed steady with the current. Banks of earth either side of you. A branch of a tree or a thorn bush dipped low over the stream, brushed against the bubble and you sitting still with no thought at how to prise them apart. Head and body full of the queer stab of joy. And that other time I saw out there for the first time, someone out there of flesh and bone and under a dark blue sky it was and the pink whitey flesh through the blue and a greeny pool of coloured light with white rims, that was eyes. I didn't know that. Instead of calling your name he slipped it in and then sucking in, letting it go, sucking it in, letting it go. Oh queer stab of joy when you saw your first blur. And he replied to you, queer stab of joy in my feet travelling down under the ground and coming up where? And the rain that day soaking me through caught my death of cold. Never been without a spit until that day and no one around, not a murmur, not even a rumble of something in the distance, why? I whirled around. Who was that? Who was there now? I whirled around. Now a tremor in you again, maybe the movement of your own feet again, for no one ever wandered by that hadn't wandered by before, it came shooting up into you, that thought. Drew a breath, let it out slowly, sharp twinge of pain running through your bones. And the leaves beginning to fall off the branches for it was Autumn time then. And the moonlight spread over the road, a pale spread of light on the patch of earth. And you twiddling your thumbs in the darkness and the occasional suck on them. Not a sound now only the breathing and the moonlight overhead in all its skulking glory. The wind breathing down your neck and you breathing in the air and the brain thinking and the heart beating and the pulse thumping and the body quite still. Body quite still now, quite, quite, still now.

It is not. It is not. Smothered in grey and bloodless out it came. It is not. It is not. Curled up or stretched skew-ways, either way a bother. Smelling of shit, demanding my nipple which promptly turned inwards. Caved in, one little brown mole collapsing before mouth could reach it. Little brown mole, little brown mole. Gaping, open mouth first sound a persistent bawling. Frying pan, frying pan, that's what I thought. Then wind. Yes that was it, rub the back. Rub the back and see will that do it. Hold it up between the knees, steady now. No frying pan still there. Out of the round gaping mouth a screaming hot sizzle. And the eyes. Blue or grey. Or maybe a mixture of green and blue. Two star-studded buttons glaring out, must have been Summer then. Sunlight in the star-studded buttons, went into a convulsion of glints and the screams grew louder. Little brown mole, around it goose pimples on grey scaly flesh. Few black hairs curling neatly, the ends barely tipping the grey scaly flesh and the veins like choking threadworms, sunlight on it all. Chair, I thought of. For no reason at all I thought, chair, chair and more chair. The whole business having started out peacefully enough, now in its usual mess. A sly thought struck me. Open knees casually and see back and screaming hole going for a slide. Water pouring out the blue grey or maybe greeny blue eyes in bucketfuls. Gasps spluttered up making back shudder, open gaping hole half closing and shutting now. Then I felt the other end letting out. All was in a collapse and the back began to quietly heave. Now no water, no screaming, all quietened down and steady stream of sunlight in through the window. Occasionally a pizzle of a sound. I opened my knees. I heard them creaking, it rolled like a rubber ball. Bounce, bounce. It, it. Not now, who? Who is it? Not me. Not now. She held my hand, jump, jump over the gorse bushes. You pale and tense and she rambling on and dragging you suddenly, 'Come on, come on,' up that hill. Not him. Not my. My who? Who? Your Daddy. Oh not me. Him. Not you. She standing by the gate, the window, breathing on the window.

'Ben. Ben, come here this minute. I'm not feelin' well. Slip down to the shop and get me a small whiskey. Tell her I've a cold coming on.'

Affirmation

Six months in the slammer and I'm powerful as ever. It takes six screws to keep me on the inside, am I or am I not doing them a service? Without me their families would starve and their relations would be kept very busy turning the blind eye. And so it goes on. I can't be kept in. I can't be put down. Even if they have to bury me I'll still be doing them a favour. Dig, dig, you hound dogs. This country is in my debt. The organisation is in my debt. Your mother, you and the other two boys are in my debt. But will you all admit it? Will you own up to the favour I have done for you? I see myself as an institution. I have become big business. The papers had a field day reporting it, they said I slit the man's throat but it's not my style. Daniel produced a knife from the inside pocket of his raincoat the night before the Big Day.

'When you're finished with it bury it,' he said.

I looked carefully over the knife and I looked back at him and said, 'What do you take me for, a butcher?'

'But you said no gun?'

'Correct. I'm not one for blowing the shit out of people.' I showed him my hands and said, 'See for yourself, I don't need any knife.'

He put the knife in the left hand pocket of my jacket. He squeezed my arm gently. In all the years and all the sons not one of you ever did that. The meeting was already set up for me. The target was under the impression he was meeting me at eleven thirty on Thursday the seventh October to receive some monies due to him. I was to put my hand in my pocket, take the knife out with the money and let him have it. I was to keep the money, lose the knife and good night to you. As simple as that, no it was not. I am not a man for instructions and I never will be.

Sylvester said when the body was found the organisation would take the usual responsibility for it and that would be that. He talked about the organisation the same way I do about God. He got a hard-on just talking about it. The man was in his element with guns and bombs and plans and raids and shoot-outs and knee-capping and knife-capping and more plans. The cowboy in him was riding the prairie and covering his tracks with banjo playing in the background and the sunset in the distance. He understood. He knew. I can't tell you the joy I felt standing beside him. He understood. He knew. We were like two idiots standing in the pouring rain not wanting to let the moment pass between us. Joy was in every pore of my being.

'When will I see you again?' I said.

'Let time pass,' he said. 'Be patient.'

The screws are my slaves. They have to be on their guard against me and at the same time they have to make sure I'm all right.

'How is the Missis keepin',' I asked the curly-haired one. 'She still tellin' you to fuck off with yourself?'

The son-of-a-bitch was livid.

'What about the childer',' I said putting on the gombeen.

'Ah I'd say now the poor childer could do with a bit of stick.'

The son-of-a-bitch was bursting apart at the seams. I laughed into his face whenever I saw him.

I arrived early to check the road out and get a good look at the target as he came towards me. What was there to look at? Sweet nothing. He was anxious to get it over with and that made me rear up too quickly.

'Why not pass the time of day? Are we so uncivilised that we can't open our mouths to each other now?' I said. He took two steps backwards and his eyes bulged in their sockets.

'What!'

'You hear me,' I said.

'Have you got a package for me?'

'You just want to go don't you?'

'Eh?'

'You don't want to talk do you? You just want the package. That's the only reason you came along here tonight.'

'Have you got the package?'

'You know what that makes you. It makes you an animal.'

'I was told to be here at eleven thirty.'

'Beg dog, beg for it.'

'I was told.'

I was told . . . I was told . . . I lunged at the son-of-a-bitch. He was half my weight and scared shitless. As I was squeezing his throat I could see the relief in his eyes. I could see the shame and guilt and relief it was all over. He struggled. I pressed harder, squeezing tightly and warmly on his throat, his eyes struggling to get out of his head, his hands beating here and there at me. Once I am concentrated on something I can't be stopped. Once I stop thinking I am freed from holding onto myself. I could feel his throat under my hands. I loved him. I adored him. I can give him no higher praise than that. He collapsed on the ground. I dragged him into the gateway of an old house and laid him down behind the hedge.

'It's all in a good cause,' I whispered to him. It tickled my fancy to talk to a dead man. Had I had the time I'd have stayed on chatting for hours. I felt as young as you son walking away from him. Now that can't be bad can it? We are not father and son, but two sons. Is there one who will love me? Is there one who will call me by my name? Who pulled the plug on me? Was it your mother? Was it you? Was it Sylvester, lovely Sylvester turning into an informer. You can see where I'm leading to, the earth is round, we go around and around with it. Just think what men and women are saying to each other every night the world over.

'Did the earth move for you my lovely?'

See what I mean, an informer is only following the laws of nature. Sylvester, Sylvester I forgive you. I am a happy man. Here I am and here I'm staying. Who pulled the plug on me?

I stood by the front window. I was cold. The spasms had passed and I had vomited, I was empty but calm. The black fist stuck in the pit of my stomach was gone. I don't know how I knew but I did know that me and Ben were out of danger. I did not want to kill myself. I did not hate myself any longer. I felt as if something had been washed out of me leaving me clean and calm. I remember the same feeling just after the Second World War was over though I think the men came home weary from it because they didn't know when to stop. Too much of anything is bad for you.

I would have used a knife on *him*. I would have gladly slit his throat. When he finally arrived home he broke out into a rant about his country, politics and religion with his glass-crunching voice about the plight of the working man. Oh yes, I thought all that and much more but you know the pleasure of it and that's what drove you to it. He finally had all the arguments sorted out and I can't say I differed with him but it's surprising how you lose interest after a blood-letting. He never actually said what he'd done but he was that excited I knew it couldn't be another woman. His whole face was flushed and glazed with lust and I was so calm and empty inside I could see the remains of the hysteria still pumping about inside him. His body looked like one big pulsating muscle and his eyes that of an eager child who has just thrown itself at its mother's feet. I hoped he wasn't going to be tiresome. There's nothing I despise more than the hypocrisy of confession.

Still and all I felt back to myself and I had him to thank so I listened politely while he talked his way around and I never once said, 'Get to the point,' because of course I knew the whole point was not to. I held myself in check and nodded here and there, waiting patiently for him to wear himself down. The lust was still throbbing through him and he looked at one stage as if he could go on about politics all night long. Mostly he lectured, this should be done, that should be done. Change this, that and the other. I never saw him attempt to change anything in his life and there he was on his soap box and I praying he wouldn't notice the boredom written all over me. I thought he'd never stop talking but eventually he did and I pressed a cup of tea into his hand.

'Drink up,' I said, 'It'll do you good.'

We sat opposite each other and I felt my old gentle self as I reassured and consoled him with such tenderness that tears sprang to my eyes.

'Why can't it always be like this,' I said.

He reached out for my hand and patted it and with one finger explored the shape of it as if for the first time. And then he drew me closer and with his other hand explored my face. And then I took my hand and reaching out cupped his face and kissed him full on the mouth. We sat holding each other, not talking, just holding and rubbing against each other and nuzzling into one another all the while he was undressing me and I him and we lay on the floor by the fire, his penis stiff and erect and I fondled his balls, I read somewhere that that helps to stop a man coming too soon, until at last I felt him slide and push inside me and he moved in and out taking me with him until I could hold on no longer and I came with him, whirling together in space our bodies rocking in slapping silent motion. Afterwards he stood up, dressed himself and scratching his head said, 'What came over me atall atall.'

I was warm. As I stood up he glanced over his shoulder at me and laughed before going on upstairs to bed.

'Don't forget to leave the light on for Ben,' he said.

I turned and whirled, oh come my lady dance, oh come my lady send my lover back home to me.

Deserts

I got myself dickied up in my best pair of jeans, orange-coloured shirt and denim jacket. Now that I was going into show business I didn't want to spoil my image so I'd given up nicking things. I came downstairs and marched into the kitchen to see what effect I'd have on her. Her head spun around like the pumpkin face on halloween and her body stiff as a stick held her spinning head.

'Well I'm off,' I said.

'Off? Where?'

'I'm goin' to join a band. How do I look?'

She shook her head as if she couldn't believe what she was seeing. 'Is that my son?' she said.

'I look smart eh!'

She nodded. 'Where's your Da?'

'He's in the slammer,' I said. 'Don't you remember, they came to the door looking for him.'

I went over and got myself a glass of water and gargled into the sink to freshen my throat. 'I look alright then?'

'You look you . . . prison you say?'

'Yeah well you were here weren't you?'

'Was I? I wonder what it's like?'

'He loves it anyway. Daddy loves everything.'

I went over to the mirror above the fireplace and stared in wonder. I looked sensational.

'This band, it's alright is it?'

'Yeah it's fine. That letter I got from Da yesterday, you want to know what's in it?'

'No I don't,' she said.

'It says he's been transferred to the hospital. He's got cancer after all.'

'Don't mind him, he's a liar. He was always a rotten liar.'

I left the house whistling softly to myself. It's nice living alone with my Ma it is.

I watched the boy with his hair black like a raven's through the front window of his house before knocking on the door. He had a red check shirt that opened out at the neck. A medallion swung loosely around his neck. They had the drums all set up on the sitting room floor and an electric guitar stood against the wall by the fireplace. He was saying something to the other fellow and he laughed, showing off a set of pure white even teeth. His pearly teeth sank softly into the side of my neck, he smelt of aftershave and sweat and his flashing eyes danced up at me as he cut into my flesh and then he sucked lovingly on his dinner. I went back to the front door and knocked and before he answered I could hear the sweet sounds of my voice soaring like a bird over the rooftops.

LANNAN SELECTIONS

The Lannan Foundation, located in Santa Fe, New Mexico, is a family foundation whose funding focuses on special cultural projects and ideas which promote and protect cultural freedom, diversity, and creativity.

The literary aspect of Lannan's cultural program supports the creation and presentation of exceptional English-language literature and develops a wider audience for poetry, fiction, and nonfiction.

Since 1990, the Lannan Foundation has supported Dalkey Archive Press projects in a variety of ways, including monetary support for authors, audience development programs, and direct funding for the publication of the Press's books.

In the year 2000, the Lannan Selections Series was established to promote both organizations' commitment to the highest expressions of literary creativity. The Foundation supports the publication of this series of books each year, and works closely with the Press to ensure that these books will reach as many readers as possible and achieve a permanent place in literature. Authors whose works have been published as Lannan Selections include Ishmael Reed, Stanley Elkin, Ann Quin, Nicholas Mosley, William Eastlake, and David Antin, among others.